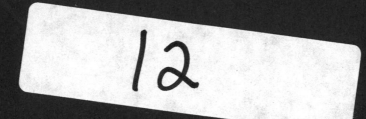

CLASS DISMISSED

ALSO BY ALLAN WOODROW

The Pet War

CLASS DISMISSED

ALLAN WOODROW

SCHOLASTIC PRESS | NEW YORK

Library of Congress Cataloging-in-Publication Data

Woodrow, Allan, author.
    Class dismissed / Allan Woodrow.—First edition.
        pages cm
    Summary: Class 507 is terrible, and one day, after a particularly disastrous science experiment, Ms. Bryce quits and walks out in the middle of class, and the school office never finds out—at first all the fifth graders enjoy goofing off, but after a few days that starts getting boring, and the students begin to realize that school without a teacher is not easy, cooperating is difficult, and keeping a secret is harder than they thought.
    ISBN 978-0-545-80071-6
    1. Elementary schools—Juvenile fiction. 2. Teachers—Juvenile fiction. 3. Secrecy—Juvenile fiction. 4. Cooperativeness—Juvenile fiction. [1. Schools—Fiction. 2. Teachers—Fiction. 3. Secrets—Fiction. 4. Cooperativeness—Fiction. 5. Humorous stories.] I. Title.
    PZ7.W86047Cl 2015
    813.6—dc23
    [Fic]

                                                                        2014048233

10 9 8 7 6 5 4 3   16 17 18 19

Printed in the U.S.A.   23
First edition, November 2015

Book design by Yaffa Jaskoll

TO MY TEACHERS, WHO INSPIRED ME, ENCOURAGED ME, AND, THANKFULLY, NEVER QUIT

1

KYLE

I look up at the clock. There's still an hour left until the school bell rings and class is dismissed.

Actually, there are sixty-four minutes and eleven seconds left.

Now, sixty-three minutes and forty-four seconds.

It's only Monday and I'm already looking forward to the weekend.

I want to raise my voice and yell, "Let me go home! Yow! Yow! Yow!"

Yow. Yow. Yow. That's what my favorite cartoon character, Squiggle Cat, always says when he's annoyed or angry or just wants to shout something.

Now there are sixty-three minutes and twenty-one seconds remaining in class.

Yow. Yow. Yow.

Don't get me wrong. School isn't totally awful. But learning is hard, and Ms. Bryce doesn't make it any easier.

Just this morning I walked up to her desk with my math sheet and said, "Ms. Bryce, I don't understand why—"

She didn't even let me finish, she just barked, "Before you add fractions, you need a common denominator." She jabbed her finger on my paper.

"What's a denominator again?"

"Look it up!" she said with a nasty frown. And that was that. I felt stupid.

Who cares what a denominator is, anyway? Fractions are stupid, not me.

I stab my notebook with my pencil, and the tip breaks. So I lean over and grab Seth's pencil from his hand. Seth frowns at me and fishes another pencil from his desk.

The class pencil sharpener broke last week so we're supposed to bring backups, but I forgot.

I can picture my extra pencil on the kitchen counter of our apartment, right where I left it, next to the carrots Mom cut up for my lunch. I forgot those, too.

I bet if Mom put the pencil next to some cookies, I wouldn't have left it behind.

But Mom never gives me lunch dessert. That's why I always swipe one from somebody else during lunch. Usually I grab a cookie, but sometimes it's a brownie or cupcake. I'm not picky. But a lunch without dessert is like a classroom without a pencil.

Meanwhile, Ms. Bryce drones on about something. I'm not really paying attention.

My pencil tip breaks. Again. I reach over to grab Seth's pencil, again, but he turns his body to block me.

"C'mon. Give me your pencil," I whisper to Seth, holding out my palm.

"Then what am I supposed to use?" Seth asks.

"I don't know," I say. "Steal Cooper's."

"What's going on back there?" Ms. Bryce hollers way too loudly. When I look up, she's frowning and staring at me. I think screaming is Ms. Bryce's second favorite thing to do in the whole world, right after sending kids to the principal's office. "Is there a problem?"

There is a problem, but it's our teacher. She has way too many rules. Except I can't say *that*. So I just shrug and say, "No problem. Sorry."

I look up at the clock. There are now fifty-nine minutes, thirty-six seconds.

Yow. Yow. Yow.

2

SAMANTHA

I loved fourth grade last year. My best friend, Bridget, was in my class, but she moved away last summer. She loved makeup and clothes as much as I do. I really miss her. We had the best teacher last year, too. Mrs. Middleton smelled like strawberries, her blond hair was almost as pretty as mine, and she had excellent fashion sense.

Mrs. Middleton and I even owned a pair of the same shoes! I have thirty-six pairs of shoes, so we only wore the same pair on the same day once.

But Ms. Bryce, my fifth-grade teacher, doesn't wear the same shoes as me. She's a fashion nightmare. Really. I had a nightmare just last week where I was forced to wear the same shapeless mustard-yellow polyester-twill secretary jacket and skirt that she's wearing right now.

I still break out in a sweat thinking about it.

Ms. Bryce paces in front of the room while I try not to

stare at her clothes. I mean, that style might have worked fifty years ago, although I doubt it. Maybe when you're ninety-six years old, your eyesight gets so bad you can't see how terrible your clothes look.

Jasmine claims that Ms. Bryce is ninety-six, but I doubt it. She's probably way older. It's not like Jasmine has seen Ms. Bryce's birth certificate or anything. I don't even know if they had birth certificates that long ago.

I should have Daddy check. Daddy can do anything.

At least, Daddy's *money* can do anything.

"Stand up and find your vinegar!" our teacher yells. Her voice pierces through the room like static electricity. Mrs. Middleton's voice sounded like cooing doves, but Ms. Bryce's voice resembles a screeching crow. "I said to stand up!" she hollers at Kyle, who is talking to Seth and not paying attention, like usual.

Kyle has bright red hair. If you're going to horse around, you shouldn't have bright red hair that stands out like a newly painted fire engine.

Our teacher stares at him, her eyes radiating darts of grouchiness. "Or do you want detention?" she barks, spit flying from her mouth.

Ms. Bryce always spits when she talks. Not that she ever talks. She screams. You practically need an umbrella if you stand too close to her, which is why I sit in the back.

"Sorry," mumbles Kyle. He looks sincere enough, but then he turns and smirks to his friends. Ms. Bryce can't see it, but I can.

"Humph!" Ms. Bryce shouts back.

But I can't blame Kyle for smirking. I mean, Ms. Bryce is more than just a fashion disaster. She's a teaching disaster, too. I wonder if I can do anything about it.

I can try, anyway.

I think about my fashion magazines. They usually have quizzes in them, and last month one of those quizzes asked, "Do you have telepathy?" *Telepathy* is the power to make things happen with your mind. The quiz included questions like *Do you know if it's going to rain before it does?* and *Do your dreams come true?* I only got four points out of twenty (my score was *A rock is more telepathic than you*) but maybe I just had an off day. Maybe, if I think really hard, as hard as I can, I can get rid of Ms. Bryce. I close my eyes and concentrate:

Retire, retire, retire, retire, retire, retire, retire, retire, retire, retire, retire!

I open my eyes. Nope. She's still here. I guess the magazine was right about me.

I should ask Daddy to buy our school, Liberty Falls Elementary, and then he could force Ms. Bryce to retire. Daddy will buy me anything. Anything except a pony, that is. He says there's no room in our penthouse apartment.

I say we should just buy a bigger apartment.

"Now pour in the vinegar," Ms. Bryce barks. "And pay attention! I'm tired of this class always messing up."

We've built little volcanoes that will ooze lava when you add vinegar. Ms. Bryce makes her students do this every year. She's so old that her classes have probably been building volcanoes since before volcanoes existed.

You'd think building volcanoes would be sort of fun. It might be, if we had a different teacher.

"Samantha, are you going to help?" asks Giovanna, reaching over for the jar of vinegar.

"I am helping," I answer. I'm holding a notebook to take notes. You never know when things might happen that are noteworthy.

Besides, I don't want to get too close to the volcano. That lava gook could get on me. What if it splashes on my new cashmere sweater?

Giovanna probably wouldn't mind if the lava got on her clothes. She is my best friend now that Bridget is gone, but that sweater is *so* last year. And her hair is curly when everyone knows straight hair is *in*. I should loan her my flat iron.

Her brown hair is the wrong shade of brown, too. It would look nicer if she added highlights. I'm always giving her fashion tips, but they never seem to sink in.

"How much vinegar should I add?" Giovanna asks me. She's holding a spoon and a jar of vinegar that's been dyed with red food coloring.

I shrug.

We turn to Ms. Bryce, but she isn't paying attention to us. She's screaming at someone else now. The spit flies.

She's yelling at Adam Lee. It looks like he took apart the broken pencil sharpener. That is *so* Adam. He practically lives in the principal's office. He could walk there blindfolded.

Adam looks at his sneakers, wringing his hands as he tries to explain himself. His face turns from olive to white and his spiky black hair sort of droops. But Ms. Bryce won't let him say a word. She turns her back to him, scribbles a note on her detention pad, and then thrusts the paper at Adam. Now she's marching him to the door, right past me. "You can explain to Principal Klein why you enjoy destroying school property!" she barks.

Poor Adam walks out, his head low.

"I'll just dump in the whole jar," Giovanna says brightly.

"Um," I say, looking at my notebook for volcano notes. I've written none. "I think you should wait until Ms. Bryce tells us exactly how much vinegar to add."

Giovanna doesn't listen. She pours the entire jar of vinegar inside the volcano top.

It immediately gurgles, and then—

Uh-oh.

The red ooze gurgles from the top of the volcano. The blobby bubbling is pretty interesting, at first. But then it keeps coming. And coming. The red-colored liquid spurts out of the volcano, followed by a large burping river of never-ending fizz. It happens so fast. One moment everything is dry, and the next moment, fake lava washes over the aluminum tray, across the desk, and spills onto the floor in large puddles.

The vinegar stink rises from the floor and I gag.

Ms. Bryce is so busy watching Adam march out of the room and toward the principal's office that she doesn't notice what has happened. She steps backward, into the red muck.

She notices it now.

She looks down. Her shoes are half buried in red glop. I think those shoes are new since I haven't seen them before, although they are so not in style. Ms. Bryce opens her mouth, and a scream like a siren screeches out, so loud and shrill that I think it might shatter the windows. I have to cover my ears. I wouldn't be surprised if people could hear her from across the school.

I wouldn't be surprised if people could hear her from across the state.

"What did you girls do?" she cries. She raises her eyebrows, and the deep wrinkles in her forehead crease even deeper.

"I just poured in the vinegar," replies Giovanna in an almost-whisper.

Ms. Bryce jabs her finger at the empty jar. "I said to put in a quarter of a cup!"

I'm about to point out that no, she didn't say that. She didn't say anything about vinegar measurement. But I keep quiet because I don't want to get in any more trouble than I might be getting into already. Ms. Bryce's face is tomato red, or rather, fake-lava red. If this were a cartoon, she'd have little clouds of smoke puffing from her ears.

"That's it!" our teacher yells. She marches to the front of the class, red glop dripping from her sensible but fashion-poor footwear. "This is the third pair of shoes you've all ruined this month!" she shouts. But I don't think you can blame us for the other two pairs. It wasn't entirely Ryan's fault that she kicked over a bucket of mop water that shouldn't have been in the middle of the room, and it's not Cooper's fault that he dropped an egg salad sandwich on Ms. Bryce's foot.

If you yell at people, they might get nervous and drop their sandwiches. So really, ruining *that* pair of shoes was entirely Ms. Bryce's fault.

Besides, her shoes are simply awful. Our destroying them is actually doing her a favor.

Ms. Bryce doesn't think that. She picks up the phone. For a moment, I worry that she's calling the police to arrest us for ruining her shoes, and I wonder how I can explain to my parents that I need them to bail me out of prison. But she presses the button for the school office instead, which makes no sense. After a few seconds of waiting, she hollers, "This is Ms. Bryce. Tell Principal Klein that I am resigning. Effective immediately!" She hangs up.

Then she grabs her coat from behind her chair, marches across the room, and leaves, slamming the door behind her.

Maybe I have magic powers. Maybe my telepathy earlier *did* work. Maybe I'm the reason she resigned!

But I doubt it.

I guess I won't have to ask Daddy to buy the school. Not anymore. Because we just lost our teacher.

I look at Giovanna, and she looks at me. Everyone in class looks at one another, this way and that way. No one knows what to do.

The room is disturbingly quiet until my volcano gives one final, loud burp and a big nugget of red froth shoots up and lands on the sleeve of my cashmere sweater.

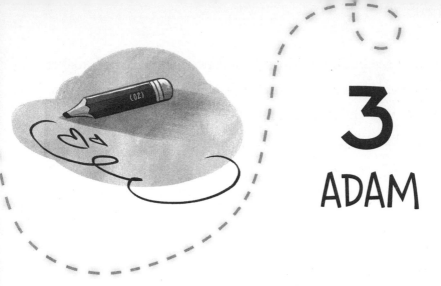

3
ADAM

Detention? Again? This is so, so unfair. I just have rotten luck, that's all. My ma and pop say that some people are born under a lucky star. But some evenings you can't see any stars, and I bet I was born on one of those nights.

In Korea, the number four is unlucky, and my birthday is April fourth. That's 4/4.

I wish I had been born in March.

But I don't deserve detention. I was doing a good deed! I was fixing something! *Trying* to fix something, anyway. Lizzie's pencil got stuck in the pencil sharpener. Everyone knows the sharpener has been broken for a week. I guess Lizzie forgot. She said that was her favorite pencil, too. It looked like any regular old pencil to me, but if it was special to Lizzie, then it must be special.

Everything about Lizzie is special, like the freckles around her nose and her light brown hair and her perfect teeth and how she was the best singer in the fourth-grade talent show last year.

Seriously, she sings like a star.

Once I took the pencil sharpener apart, I wasn't quite sure how to put it together again. I thought it would be easy. It should have been easy. But the pieces didn't quite fit back the way they were supposed to. That's hardly my fault.

And for that, for trying to do a good deed, I get sent to the principal's office? Every day it seems like it's not *if* I'll go to his office, but *when*.

They have lollipops outside his office, in a small green metal bucket next to the sheet where parents sign in to pick up their kids. I usually grab a sucker. Maybe today I'll grab two, one for me and one for Lizzie. A lollipop is better than a pencil. You can't lick a pencil. Well, I suppose you can lick anything, but a pencil wouldn't taste very good.

I wonder what flavor Lizzie likes. Raspberry. I bet she likes raspberry.

Or grape. I'll grab one of each.

My sneakers squeak with every step down the hallway. Everything sounds louder when you walk in the hall by yourself.

Going to the principal's office is the loneliest feeling in the world.

My sneakers go SQUEAK, SQUEAK, SQUEAK. But I pass no one.

I walk slowly. There's no sense in rushing. The longer it takes to walk to the office, the longer I won't be in trouble.

So, my sneakers sort of go:

SQUEAK.

Pause.

SQUEAK.

Pause.

SQUEAK.

When I get to the office, all the grown-ups are hurrying away, even Mrs. Frank, the school secretary. Her tall, tight, gray-hair bun doesn't sway an inch even as she dashes off.

I wonder why everyone is rushing, and if I missed a fire drill. But I would have heard *that*. Those alarms are loud. They're even louder than Ms. Bryce. And she's as thundering as a foghorn.

No one in the office sees me as they dart from their desks and across the room and into the teachers' lounge in back. The teachers' lounge door is propped open, and all of the office workers crowd inside with the art teacher, Mrs. Wilson, in the middle.

I hear Principal Klein. I couldn't miss his deep, loud voice anywhere. I hear it almost every day, although usually he starts with the words, "What did you do *this* time, Adam?"

Curious, I stand on my tiptoes to get a better look at what's happening back there.

"We'll get your necklace out, Mrs. Wilson," Principal Klein says. "It's just caught in the disposal." He rolls up his sleeve and sticks his hand in the sink.

"Maybe we should wait for the janitor . . . ," Mrs. Wilson says.

"Nonsense," Principal Klein replies, and it looks like he's pulling on the caught necklace.

His hand jerks backward, he slips, and suddenly a spout of water erupts from the sink. The wave soaks Mrs. Wilson's and Principal Klein's faces.

Principal Klein is holding the faucet in his hands. "Whoops."

While the school administration fights with the teachers' lounge sink, I wonder what I should do. Should I stay here and wait? Should I help? I could fix the sink.

I bet I'm better at fixing sinks than I am at fixing pencil sharpeners.

Then the office phone rings. Once. Twice. It's right next to me, a button flashing, demanding to be answered. "The phone is ringing!" I call out, but there's no one in the office to hear me.

Should *I* answer the phone? What if it's important? I can take a message or grab a teacher if it's an emergency. It would be a good deed to answer the phone.

Maybe I won't get in trouble for destroying the pencil sharpener if I answer the phone.

I pick up the receiver. I'm about to say something like "Liberty Falls Elementary, can I help you?" when a voice yells through the receiver. I recognize that angry bark at once.

"This is Ms. Bryce. Tell Principal Klein that I am resigning. Effective immediately!"

Before I can tell her that I'm Adam and she should hold on while I get someone else, she hangs up. The dial tone buzzes in my ear, so I put the receiver back on the base.

I look around. No one has noticed.

"Anyone have a wrench?" Principal Klein shouts from the teachers' lounge as water continues to spray into the air.

There are even more people standing around the sink now. Most of the adults seem to be dripping wet. The principal has his hands down the sink again, water continuing to drench him.

Mrs. Wilson says urgently, "Please be careful. It was a wedding gift." A couple of secretaries pat her on the shoulder.

Principal Klein steps back, the sink makes a loud grinding noise, and then an even higher geyser of water fills the air. It's like the mermaid fountain in the town pond, shooting water from her mouth.

It looks like they will be busy for a while.

So I decide to go back to class.

The halls are still empty and I feel nervous about returning to our room without saying anything to anyone in the office.

If you are sent to the office but no one knows you were sent to the office, does it really count as being sent to the office?

I hope I don't get into more trouble. Knowing my luck, I probably will.

My sneakers squeak the entire way. For sneakers, they aren't very sneaky.

When I enter the classroom, no one is talking. An eerie silence covers the room. It stinks like vinegar. I hold my breath to keep from choking.

I take my seat in the middle of class, between Lizzie and Eli. I tap Lizzie on the shoulder and hand her six lollipops. "They're from the principal's office," I explain. "I wasn't sure what flavor you liked."

She smiles at me with a big grin, her freckles shining like tiny bright fireworks on her cheeks. My heart skips a beat or two.

She smiled! At me!

I grab my pencil and begin drawing on the desk. I draw *L + A* in little hearts, and in big hearts, too. I draw about five of them when I realize—I'm drawing on the desk! I've been sent to the principal's office ten times for drawing on the desk. I can't help myself, though. The desk looks so clean.

A clean desk is begging to be doodled on. Really.

Still, I lick my thumb to rub over my drawings and erase them. I don't want our teacher to yell at me.

But then I stop and look down at a now half-erased, smudged heart.

Ms. Bryce won't yell. She's not even here.

She just quit.

I can do anything—*anything at all!*—and no one will send me to the principal's office.

No more being screamed at. No more getting into trouble for no good reason.

A feeling of happiness spreads over me. I feel free.

I stand up. "Um, guys?" I say. Everyone stares at me, their eyes glaring loudly through the uncomfortable silence of the room. I clear my throat and shuffle from my right leg to my left. "I have some news." The class continues their stares. The room is so quiet you can hear the lights humming from the ceiling. "Well. See. Ms. Bryce. She resigned."

"We already know that," says Seth from the back.

"Right. Sure." I look at Lizzie, who starts to unwrap the grape-flavored lollipop I gave her. Then I look back at the rest of the class. "But. There's something I know you don't know." The class continues to watch me, silently. "You see, I'm pretty sure no one knows she resigned—except us."

No one says anything. Not a student moves. I'm about to repeat what I said, thinking maybe no one quite understood what I meant, when Brian jumps up and yells, "No one knows we don't have a teacher? Did you hear that? This is amazing! It's party time!"

4

KYLE

Yow. Yow. Yow.

Ms. Bryce is gone? Retired? Out the door and never coming back?

I jump out of my seat and smack Brian's raised hand with a powerful, high-speed, all-star high five.

Brian returns my smack with one that's even harder. His smack hurts.

Brian's big—he's even bigger than me. A hand slap from Brian is worth about five slaps from anyone else.

But he could smash my hand a hundred times and this would still be the greatest day in the history of greatest days.

We're going to talk loudly. Chew gum. And do anything we want, whenever we want.

We'll toss spit wads and topple chairs.

We'll play games and pull girls' hairs.

At least until we get a new teacher.

I think of a few more rhymes, which is something I like to sometimes do, although I don't tell Brian and Seth about it. They would say only girls like poetry and think I was a sissy. Anyway, here are the rhymes that I think:

Playing is great and candy is nice,
But best thing of all? No more Ms. Bryce!

And also:

Slap my hand, we're all enthusiastic.
Ms. Bryce is gone! And that's fantastic.

Seth is behind me, palm up and ready for a jam-packed hand slap. His palm meets mine. CRACK! Seth is the same size as me, so it doesn't hurt as much as Brian's slap.

Yes, this is the greatest of days.

Yow. Yow. Yow.

Last night something happened that was pretty awesome, too. While Mom was changing my baby brother AJ's diapers, I saw a letter sticking out of her purse. I couldn't help reading it since it was sticking out and all. Letters that stick out of things demand to be read.

It was from the accounting company where Mom works. She was offered a promotion. Which means maybe we could move into a bigger apartment. We've been stuck in the same one ever since Dad left. Even with one less person it's awfully cramped with the five of us kids.

When I asked Mom when she'd start her new position, she

gave me a lecture about going through her stuff. And then she said that she didn't know if she would accept the promotion.

Which is crazy, right? Of course she should accept it!

But you know what's even crazier? Having school without having a teacher. This might even be better than Mom's letter.

Brian and Seth are still jumping up and down and hooting. I hoot, too. We stomp our feet. We pound our desks.

But not everyone hops and hollers and desk-pounds. Maggie, in the front row, wears a strange frown. She's whispering to Lacey, who frowns, too.

They look disappointed about our awesome news.

I guess that makes sense, though. Ms. Bryce didn't like anyone, but she never punished any of those front-row-seat-sitting, glasses-wearing, know-it-all girls.

Only the class brains sit in the front row, and teachers always like the class brains.

"We should tell someone, right?" asks Gavin.

Brian, Seth, and I stop jumping.

Tell someone?

Brian pounds the table. His voice is low and threatening. "No way. We keep quiet." He cracks his knuckles. "It'll be the most amazing fifth-grade secret ever."

Yow. Yow. Yow.

We won't have a teacher for the rest of the entire year? Is that even possible?

I want to slap everyone's hand, even Soda's paw. Soda, our classroom hamster, sits in the corner of his cage, watching us. His little golden ears prick up, and his nose twitches. I bet you that he can tell something exciting is happening.

He's smart, for a hamster.

"But how are we going to learn?" asks Maggie, raising her voice. I turn away from Soda to look at her. "We go to school to *learn*, remember?"

"I want to learn," says Paige, standing on one side of Maggie.

"Me too," says Lacey. She stands on Maggie's other side.

Lacey and Paige and Maggie don't really look alike, but they all wear the same thick, round glasses. They look like three owls. Three smart owls.

Of course the owls want to learn. Learning comes easy to them. But what about the rest of us?

What about me?

See you, science. Good-bye, reading. Math, go away!

The only things we want to learn are new games to play.

I step forward. "We're not here to learn," I insist. "We go to school because our parents want us out of the house for a few hours."

"I know mine do," agrees Seth.

"We have to go to school," snaps Maggie. "It's the law."

"But it's not the law to *learn*," I argue. "Who says we can't have fun instead?"

"Let's have fun!" shouts Brian. He and Seth bang their fists on their desks. Brian lets loose a loud, "Booyah!"

But not every kid looks convinced. Jade and Eli frown. The twins, Danny and Jasmine, have confused, faraway stares, as if they don't know whether to applaud or run into the halls screaming for a teacher.

"Let's vote," I suggest. "We'll decide as a class if we should tell the principal our teacher quit, or keep quiet."

A few students shout their agreement. Others keep their uncertain gazes. Brian yells, "Vote! Vote! Vote!" and then he adds, "And you better vote for keeping your mouths shut."

Maggie clears her throat and steps forward so she's standing in front of the whiteboard. She faces us, removes her glasses, wipes her lenses on her shirt, and then puts her glasses back on. "My fellow students," she says, her chin up as if she's running for president of the United States or something. "Let me remind you of the importance of our education. How can we expect to do well at Liberty Falls Middle School next year? Or graduate as high school valedictorians? And go to college, without a solid education? The short answer: We won't!"

"I don't want to be a valedictorian!" Brian hoots, and then he adds, quieter, "Whatever that is."

"Can I still become a stylist?" asks Emmy. "I want to work in my mom's hair salon when I'm older."

"No!" says Maggie, forming a fist and pounding on her open palm, like a hammer to a nail. "Without an education, we are all doomed to lives of failure. My parents say that brains are like babies. Just like a baby needs food and love to grow big and healthy, our brains need reading and studying. Brains don't grow from shouting and jumping around, but from learning and homework and tests."

"Tests?" says Brian. "Are you crazy?" Seth joins him in a chorus of hisses aimed at Maggie.

I give Maggie credit, though. She doesn't budge. Instead she purses her lips.

Maggie raises her voice even louder to shout over the boos raining from Brian and Seth. "I know that teachers have super-easy jobs. I know that it *seems* like playing games all day would be fun. But without homework, our futures are doomed."

"Boo!" I call. "Boo to homework!"

Surprisingly, Madelyn boos, too, and so does Jade. They usually participate in class. They always raise their hands.

I guess people can surprise you sometimes.

The boos are contagious. They start to spread like the flu, until half the class is shouting them.

Trevor says to Maggie, "Sit down, Miss Bossy."

"Vote! Vote! Vote!" yells Brian.

Maggie frowns and opens her mouth to speak, but the boos drown out whatever she says.

Suddenly, I realize how loud we're being. "Keep it down, or the other classes will hear!" I warn.

Whoops. I shouldn't have screamed that.

But the class quiets. The walls are thick. I just don't know *how* thick. "Who wants to tell the principal we need a teacher?" I ask. "Raise your hand if you want to blab and ruin everything."

Maggie raises her hand immediately, but no one else joins her. Hers is the lone raised arm until she glares at Lacey and Paige. They slowly lift their hands, too. Neither looks happy about it.

Even the brains aren't convinced we should talk.

Some other kids half raise their arms, but Brian snaps a pencil in two and looks around the room. The message is clear: Raise your hand at your own risk.

No other arm rises.

"And who thinks we should keep quiet?" I ask.

Brian and Seth lift their arms as if they've been shot out of two cannons. Just about everyone else in class follows their lead.

A few kids don't vote, and Brian cracks his knuckles again. Three more hands shoot into the air. I think one kid didn't vote, but it's pretty clear which side has won.

It's not even close.

"It looks like we're keeping quiet," I say.

"But we can't—" says Maggie.

"Stop acting like a third grader," snaps Trevor. A couple of kids laugh. Maggie sits down. She folds her arms and frowns, but doesn't say a word.

"So we can't tell anyone. *Anyone*," I say. "Agreed? Not your parents. Not your brother or sister. And not even your best friend. Our secret can't leave this room."

"Swear on the Smelly Sock!" orders Brian. He reaches into his backpack and pulls out an old white tube sock that's stiff and crusty with mud, bird poop, and who knows what else.

The room gasps.

I forgot Brian still had the Smelly Sock. It's really disgusting. There's a whole story about it—a whole, really gross, practically vomit-worthy story about it.

Two years ago, we found the sock in the bushes outside school. It might have been hiding there for years. We kept it and we formed a Smelly Sock Club. You had to declare allegiance to the Smelly Sock and kiss it. If you didn't, it meant you hated socks, and if you hated socks, it meant your feet smelled like a smelly sock.

I'm not sure if that made sense, but it seemed to at the time. Only one kid refused to pucker up.

His family moved away last year, and I'm pretty sure it's because everyone in school called him Smelly Sock Scott. (I don't even think his name was Scott.)

Looking back, I feel sort of bad about what we did. Brian likes to pick on some of the kids, and sometimes it's fun to join in. But I don't know. Other times it just feels sort of . . . not right.

Brian waves the sock in the air and the entire class swears on it, including Maggie and the other brains and the one non-voting kid—

He's a scrawny, quiet kid with short rust-colored hair. I usually forget he's even there. I think his name is Eric.

"This is going to be awesome!" says Seth.

We won't tell a soul, no way, no how.

We'll all keep our secret. Yow. Yow. Yow!

Brian puts the sock back into his backpack, crammed between his notebooks and pencil case. I can't believe he carries that thing around with him every day.

I'll have to avoid his backpack. It must smell really, really horrible.

The class grows quiet and watches me, as if they expect me to start assigning homework or something.

But this isn't about homework. It's about *not* homework.

"What do we do now?" asks Madelyn. She's tall and thin, and her voice reminds me of a helium balloon.

"Play!" yells Brian, chucking an eraser at me.

5

ERIC

I sit on my chair watching the class celebrate. The Big Goofs—that's what I call Kyle, Brian, and Seth—chuck erasers at one another. Other kids huddle in groups talking loudly about who knows what, or jumping around like they have jumping beans in their shoes. I sit by myself, watching them.

I was the only kid who didn't vote on whether we should tell the principal our incredible news. And I stuck out like a giant nose pimple, one giant unpopped nose pimple. I should have voted. I should have raised my hand high and voted for keeping quiet.

It's funny. I hate raising my hand because I don't like being noticed. But this time I was noticed because I *didn't* raise my hand. That's called *irony*.

Irony is when the opposite of what you expected to have happen ends up happening, anyway. Like when the teacher asks a question and you try to slink low in your chair so she doesn't see you, but then she calls on you simply because she saw you slink low in your chair.

There's a thin line between not being noticed and being noticed for trying not to be noticed. It's an art to blend in, keep quiet, and keep your head down, while avoiding obvious eye-catching and unintended ironic slinking.

Kyle chucks erasers at just about everyone, although mostly Brian and Seth. That's the good thing about blending in. No one thinks to chuck erasers at you.

Still, I worry about our class secret. I see nothing but potential problems.

Who will sit in on our parent-teacher conferences next month? Who will give us grades and report cards? Who will line us up for lunch?

Our principal—and if not him, then someone—is going to discover our secret, and when he does, we'll all be in a giant mountain of mess.

We're going to get caught. We're going to get in trouble. We're going to be punished.

Man oh man, are we going to be punished.

We'll get detention for a year. Be kicked out of school. Be forced to eat beef nachos every day for lunch, a food I've never actually eaten but looks frightening in the cafeteria lunch line. I bet even the lunch ladies have never tried it. I think some crabby old man lurks in the back of the cafeteria inventing the worst foods he can imagine and then serves them to us kids, with beef nachos his crowning achievement.

I've heard rumors that the beef in the beef nachos is made from frog meat. That's probably not true, but I'm not taking any chances.

I should write a story about the beef nachos. It would be a horror story.

An eraser hits Jade on the shoulder. Madelyn sings. Cooper looks through the supply cabinet, probably searching for our teacher's secret supply of snacks. I take out my notebook to write a story.

One of the best things about writing is you don't have to talk to anyone or worry about doing something stupid. As soon as your pencil starts moving, you're lost in your own brain, where you can write anything you can think. And if you make a mistake, no one knows and no one cares. You can just erase what you wrote and start over again.

I start to write about beef nachos, but then quickly change my mind and begin writing a short story about a classroom just like mine. I call it "The Flower Children."

In my story, kids goof off and never listen to their teacher, Mrs. Brick. She tells the kids to pay attention, but they ignore her. Finally, Mrs. Brick has had enough. No one knows that she's a witch! She raises her wand and turns all the students into flowers.

All the loud kids are loud, colorful flowers. The big kids are giant flowers. But one kid, a quiet kid who no one ever noticed, is a small, dull, nothing stem.

Later that night, the principal walks into the class and spies flowers growing next to each desk. *Those will make a beautiful bouquet for my wife*, he thinks, and picks them.

The large and bright flowers quickly get picked. But the principal doesn't even notice that one boring plant.

The next morning the spell wears off. The quiet kid wakes up at his desk. The other kids wake up in the principal's house next to a broken vase and a small puddle of water that ruins the carpeting. Their principal refuses to believe they were flowers and suspends them all from school. Only the quiet kid avoids trouble.

I look up from my story and gaze around the classroom. I was so busy writing that I lost track of what everyone else was doing.

Adam draws on his desk. Emmy and Eli write on the whiteboard. Jade and Madelyn dance on their desks. They'd better be careful that they don't get hurt—there's no way they can go to the school nurse without our secret leaking out.

With a wad of paper and a trash can, Trevor and Gavin play basketball. They both wear matching basketball jerseys every day, so I guess they love the sport. Maggie and the brains thumb through the teacher's files. Cooper eats a candy bar and burps. I think part of the bar has melted, since his hands are covered in chocolate. He wipes his fingers on his desk.

Everyone is breaking about a dozen class rules.

Or rather, they are breaking our *old* class rules. There are no longer any class rules to break. Not anymore.

"I'm going to open the door!" announces Ryan. She wears a baseball hat, which is against another rule: No wearing hats in school. Or rather, that *was* a rule. "It reeks in here." As she walks, she spins in circles, like a dancer.

The volcano vinegar fumes cover the room in a blanket of gag-creating stink. I forgot about the smell while I wrote, but now that Ryan mentions it, the odor bombards my nostrils.

I pinch them shut.

But before Ryan can open the door, Kyle yells out, "Wait!"

Everyone stops what he or she is doing and turns to stare at Kyle.

"It's just . . . ," he begins. "It's just that I bet the smell will keep teachers away from our class. We should keep the door closed and let the smell stink people away, at least for a few days. It'll just seep through the crack under the door and last longer that way."

I would have thought Kyle was incapable of a good idea, but he's right. We should keep the lingering smell if we want to be safe. No one wants to enter a room that reeks of vinegar.

It's a pretty big idea from a Big Goof. I'm surprised. I didn't know the Big Goofs ever had big ideas.

Ryan spins back to her seat, leaving the door closed, and Kyle hurtles an eraser at her feet. It appears that Kyle is back to being a goof.

I wonder how long we'll keep the secret, though. Someone is going to spill it.

But I know I won't say a word to anyone. After all, I find it easy not saying a word to anyone.

I am not a colorful flower. I will remain quiet and planted—right on my seat.

6

KYLE

The apartment building hallway smells of curry, and the odor gets stronger and stronger as I hurry past apartment 3F. I want to fling open their door and tell Mrs. Singh, who's probably inside cooking dinner, "My teacher quit! My teacher quit!"

I imagine running down the entire hall screaming at the top of my lungs.

Someone would probably yell at me to stop running in the halls.

But I can't say a word, anyway. I'm sworn to secrecy. It's hard to keep secrets. And yow, yow, yow, do I have an epic secret.

This afternoon was fantastic. We played Eraser Wars, which is a game Seth, Brian, and I made up, and threw Lacey's book back and forth while she shouted at us to stop. I just laughed, but at the same time I was laughing, a small voice inside my brain kept telling me that this was all too good to be true. *Come on!* said the voice. *You can't goof off for the rest of the year.*

Shut up, I told that voice. *Why not? Go away! Let me goof!*

We have to keep our traps shut. That's all, and then nothing will go wrong.

So I march down my apartment hallway without banging on doors and without hollering my secret to everyone in the building.

As soon as I open my door, Nate rams into my leg. "Be careful, little guy," I say.

My almost-four-year-old brother wears a blue superhero cape but nothing else. He bounces up off the ground and runs into the kitchen, calling, "I'm Captain Nate!"

"You go, superhero," I say with a laugh.

In the kitchen, two-year-old Leah sits on the floor banging pots and pans. CRASH! BIM! TANG! Nate sits down and joins her in the mayhem.

Mom yells from a back bedroom, "Kyle? Is that you? Can you take out the garbage and put the pizza in the oven for dinner? I'm going to give AJ a bath and then put him to bed!"

I want to ask if she's taken that promotion yet. When she does, and we move to a bigger apartment, I hope I'll finally get my own bedroom. I'm sick of sharing one with Nate.

"In a minute!" I yell. I walk back into the hallway and close the front door, which I accidentally left open. Mom hates when I do that. In the family room, my six-year-old sister, Marley, watches cartoons. "Move over, Squirt," I tell her.

She frowns but wiggles over.

I drop my backpack on the floor. For the first time in forever there is no homework inside it, and no tests to study for. I spread my arms and smile. This is how prisoners must feel when they are let out after months or years of being locked away.

Freedom! I lean back on the couch.

"Twenty years!" cried the judge. The crook sobbed, "You're too cruel."

The judge shrugged. "Could be worse. I could send you to school."

On the television screen, Squiggle Cat gets poked in the eye. He yells, "Yow! Yow! Yow!" I stretch out my legs and laugh.

The show is an hour long, with lots of short episodes. Each is funnier than the last one.

"How long until the pizza's done?" Mom yells from a bedroom.

When I hear my mom, I sit up. The pizza. Dinner. "I'm starting it now!"

I spring off the couch.

Back in the kitchen, Leah and Nate have grown bored with pot banging and are hitting the floor with a pair of wooden spoons. Leah hits my leg with the spoon, and I growl at her, like a bear. I raise my arms as if they are claws and bend down. "Roar!" She laughs and hits me again with the spoon.

I suppose she thinks I'm more the teddy bear than the grizzly bear type. I doubt most of the kids in school would agree with her, though.

A commercial blares from the family room television. I need to get the pizza in the oven and my butt back on the couch fast. I don't want to miss the show.

I take the pizza from the freezer. The directions are on the box. Preheat the oven. Put in the pizza. Set the timer.

Easy.

I turn on the oven and then—

Wait. Stop. Take a breath.

Mom needs two chores done. What was the other one?

The garbage. Right.

The trash smells like it hasn't been emptied in days. Then I remember that Mom asked me to do it yesterday, but I forgot.

"The show is back on!" Marley says from the family room.

"Yow, yow, yow!" yells Squiggle Cat.

I'm a blur of action. I grab the garbage bag and heave. The top of the plastic bag tears, but I slide it out, anyway. I cram the pizza carton inside, although it doesn't fit so well. But it's only garbage. It doesn't have to look neat.

"You're missing the show!" yells Marley.

"I know!" I holler back.

The garbage chute is all the way at the other end of the hallway, so I'll walk the trash down later. After dinner. Or after that.

I place the bag in the hallway. Then I hurry back to the kitchen, toss the pizza in the oven, set the timer for exactly eighteen minutes, and bang, bang, I plop back on the couch just as Squiggle Cat gets poked in the eye. "Yow, yow, yow!" he screams.

It's a funny show. Marley and I roll over on the couch, laughing. I close my eyes to take a short, happy nap.

"What's that smell?" Mom asks a few minutes later. Or maybe it's a lot later. I pop open my eyes. A strong, burning plastic stink streams from the kitchen. The oven timer is buzzing.

Mom dashes through the hall and into the kitchen. Then she's yelling words that, if I said them, would get me grounded for a week. I jump up from the couch and peek into the kitchen.

Smoke swirls and it would probably set off our smoke alarm if I had changed the batteries like Mom asked a few weeks ago. The new batteries still sit on the counter, a daily reminder to put them in, which I always swear I'll do later. Mom removes the pizza from the oven, melted plastic merging with cheese, and tosses it into the sink.

I was supposed to unwrap the plastic film from the pizza before I put it into the oven.

But the directions didn't say that! At least, I don't think they did.

The timer is still ringing, and Mom turns it off. I think it must have been going off for a long time. The buzzer is hard to hear over the TV when you're napping.

"All I ask is for a little help!" Mom yells at me. And yells and yells, as if I'm not good for anything.

I *was* trying to help.

And then Leah, who's sitting on the floor gnawing on her wooden spoon, starts crying.

Mom stops screaming and bends down, wrapping little Leah in a big hug. "Look what you've done!" she snaps at me, although it was her shouting that made little Leah cry.

I stomp back to the family room, where Marley's still watching TV. I walk with loud, angry stomps. I bet our neighbors downstairs can hear me, their ceiling shaking under my footsteps.

I just wish I could snap my fingers and be back in school. My friends don't act like I'm good for nothing. They don't care if I can't follow a few stupid directions.

Now, without a teacher, I won't have to worry about following directions in school again, anyway. I can do whatever I want, whenever I want.

Without a teacher, we won't have any rules, which sounds perfectly awesome to me.

7
MAGGIE

I'm in a class of blockheads. Really, truly, and absolutely. Lacey and Paige are not, certainly, but they are the exceptions. Or, maybe, probably, they are only semi-blockhead-ish, say 35 percent blockhead and 65 percent not.

I can't believe we haven't had a teacher since yesterday and have agreed to keep this inconceivable secret for maybe the entire year.

Inconceivable. That means unbelievable, extraordinary, and totally preposterous. The kids in class have lost their collective minds, if they even had minds. I'm guessing they didn't.

All the kids in class *combined* equal maybe one mind.

Or maybe their minds are just made out of blocks, ergo *blockheads.*

But I promised to keep quiet, too. And all because I was afraid of a smelly sock? I'm as big of a blockhead as everyone else.

It's taken all my willpower to keep from marching down to Principal Klein's office and demanding a new teacher, *now*.

But a vow is a vow is a vow.

Which is the same as a promise, an agreement, an oath, a binding oral contract between the blockheads and me.

And a smelly sock is a smelly sock is a smelly sock.

I don't smell like a sock, even if the whole idea is ludicrous and makes no sense. Are we supposed to like socks, hate socks, or what?

Besides, everyone already thinks I'm the teacher's pet. So I just had to go with the majority. I didn't have a choice.

I started to object, I really did, but then Trevor whispered to Gavin, and not very softly, that "of course Little Miss Bossy has a problem," and then he called me the same thing out loud to everyone, so I couldn't say anything.

Still, this changes everything. And I mean *everything*! No teacher means no more teaching, no more teaching means no more learning, and no more learning means falling behind in school and having a life of miserable mediocrity.

I, Maggie Cranberry, refuse to lead a life of mediocrity, thank you very much.

I have my life planned out—perfectly planned out on a spreadsheet on my computer. After excelling throughout my secondary schooling, I will graduate number one in our high school class: top of the ladder, chief genius, and VIP of scholarly smartness. Then I move right on to Harvard—a full scholarship, naturally. Mom and Dad went to Harvard, and so did my aunts and uncles. They expect me to go, too. I won't let them down. I won't be the first Cranberry to fail.

My great-great-great-uncle was only the fourth African American to graduate from Harvard, too! Or maybe he was the seventh one to graduate. Top ten, for sure.

Paige tells me I worry about college too much since we're only in fifth grade.

With that attitude, you can be sure *she's* not getting into Harvard.

Paige also tells me that I need to relax. I tell her that I can relax when I'm old, like when I'm twenty-five.

But all of my plans are now in jeopardy. How am I supposed to learn without a teacher?

Teaching kids has to be one of the easiest jobs in the world, too. To teach first grade, you just need to reach second grade. And anyone who has reached third grade can easily teach second grade, and so on, and so on.

As a fifth grader, I'm practically overqualified to be a teacher.

And—and this is a humongous *and*—when you're a teacher, kids do all the work while teachers just grade and judge it. How easy is that?

I brought a math textbook to school today. I'm going to learn, even if no one else will. Let the other kids waste their time and their brain cells. My teachers say I'm a go-getter. So I'll just go get myself an education.

Lacey and Paige chat. They brought their textbooks, like I told them to do. They were planning on bringing games to class, and I reminded them we needed to set an example.

But Lacey and Paige are helpless. Are they studying? No! They're talking about boys and television and other monumental wastes of time.

Although a couple of the boys in class are cute, sort of.

Paige asks me, "On TV last night, did you watch—"

My eyes narrow into slits. "No, I did not *watch TV* last night. I read."

The rest of the class ignores their minds as completely and ridiculously as Lacey and Paige disregard theirs. Cooper brought a pile of comic books, which he shares with Gavin and Trevor.

A waste.

In the corner, Samantha braids Giovanna's hair.

More waste.

In back of me, kids talk, laugh, joke, play, and doodle. Jasmine and Danny, the twins, make paper fortune-tellers.

Waste, waste, waste, waste, and waste.

But worst of everyone in class, Kyle hurls erasers and wrestles with his equally irritating friends. I can't think of a bigger waste than Kyle and his friends, even if I like the way Kyle's bright red hair stands up on the top of his head.

Kyle is sort of cute, in a redheaded Neanderthal sort of way.

Neanderthal means oafish, ape-like, and very, very annoying.

The room is a din of noise and commotion. Why can't kids goof off quietly? It's hard to study with all these distractions. I want to scream at them to "BE QUIET, YOU BLOCKHEADS!"

But then the class phone rings. It's loud, abrasive, surprising, and sudden—a piercing wake-up call through the lazy glaze of goofing. Everyone quiets and stares at the phone, as if it will answer itself. Of course, my desk is closest to the teacher's desk and phone. That's where I always sit so teachers notice me raising my hand to answer their questions.

The phone rings again.

I suppose *someone* has to answer the phone, or it'll ring forever. And I'll never get any work done if the phone rings forever. So, I stand up, stride to the desk, and pick up the handset. I clear my throat. "Yes?"

"Ms. Bryce, how are you?" It's Principal Klein. I recognize his deep, booming voice.

"I am terribly sorry, but I'm not—"

"I'll get right to the point, Ms. Bryce," he says, interrupting me. "We did not get your attendance sheet this morning."

"I am not—" I repeat, but then I stop. Everyone stares at me, wondering what I'll say next.

"You are not what?" asks Principal Klein.

A vow is a vow is a vow.

A smelly sock is a smelly sock is a smelly sock.

I clear my throat. I screech, so my voice sounds more like Ms. Bryce's. "I'm not sure why I didn't turn in the sheet. Everyone is here."

"And lunch?" he asks.

Right. Lunch. We forgot about lunch. Every day, Ms. Bryce writes down on the attendance sheet who will buy lunch. It's a simple routine. Yet we completely neglected to do it.

It's pretty obvious this class secret isn't going to last for long, because everyone is a blockhead, including me. But I won't be the one to blab. I gave a vow, even if the vow was moronic, inane, and completely without basic common sense.

"No one is buying lunch today," I say, my voice clipped.

"Very well," says Principal Klein. "But don't forget to turn in those sheets tomorrow."

"Of course not. Who do you think I am?"

And he hangs up.

I stand there, holding the phone. Part of me feels simply terrible for lying to the principal. I feel guilty, awful, and lower than a parasitic earthworm. My knees shake. The principal! You don't lie to *him*!

But part of me also feels giddy, joyous, and elated, as if I've just found a new dictionary under the Christmas tree. Principal Klein thought I was Ms. Bryce. He didn't suspect the truth. He assumed I was in charge.

And why not? Someone has to be in charge.

Why not me?

Maybe, just maybe, I can turn this entire ridiculous adventure to my advantage. My camp counselor last summer told my parents I was a natural-born leader. Ivy League colleges love leaders.

If I take charge of this class, then *that* will look impressive on my Harvard application. I'll make Mom and Dad proud, just you wait and see.

The other kids might say I'm too serious, but we're all going to start seriously learning in class again, whether anyone else wants to learn or not.

8

ERIC

I sit at my desk with my pencil, notebook, and a copy of *Hamlet*, the book I brought to class. A few other kids brought books, but no one reads one.

I open my book. *Hamlet* isn't a book, really, it's a play by Shakespeare, who most people say was the greatest playwright ever. Shakespeare lived a long time ago, and it's hard to read his plays because he uses a whole bunch of words I've never heard of before.

I can't read more than a few lines at a time without my mind swimming in confusion.

Like this line: "I am but mad north-north-west: when the wind is southerly I know a hawk from a handsaw."

Huh?

But Shakespeare is supposed to be brilliant, and if I want to be a brilliant writer, I need to read brilliant things, even if they are impossible to understand.

Meanwhile, around the room, everyone seems bored.

A group of girls sit in a circle and Madelyn tells a story about her cat. I think it's the fourth time she's told the same story. Pieces of familiar conversation float across the room to me.

Eli made a giant paper-clip chain but has run out of paper clips, so he walks around trying to borrow some from everyone.

"I don't have any paper clips," I say.

"Are you sure?" he asks. "It's important."

"Yeah. Sorry."

Right in front of me, Adam and Lizzie sit on the floor, doodling on the backs of their chairs. Their desks are completely doodled over, so I suppose they ran out of room on them.

Adam brushes his arm against Lizzie's and then pretends it's an accident. But I don't think it's an accident.

You can get to know people pretty well just from watching them.

Danny, who sits to my left, rests his head on his desk, yawning widely. Next to him, Jasmine rests her head, too, and snores lightly. Behind them, Kyle takes a break from throwing erasers to feed our room hamster, Soda. I'm glad someone remembered to feed it. He closes the container of hamster food and then hurls an eraser at Jasmine's head. She lurches up from her nap, annoyed. The eraser sticks in her thick dreadlocks. She doesn't even bother to remove it, and instead she goes back to sleep.

That's the thing about school. We may have hated Ms. Bryce, but at least we had things to do. If you ever yawned or closed your eyes, she'd yell at you.

But we're stuck here and we can't leave, or someone might see us and wonder why we're not in class. Then our secret would leak for sure.

A couple of kids brought phones, but since they aren't allowed in school, most kids didn't want to risk being caught by their parents sneaking them to class.

I think Maggie is up to something, though. She sits in front at the teacher's desk, riffling through Ms. Bryce's files and old homework papers. Every few seconds she looks up, smiles, and continues browsing.

Yesterday, I thought Maggie was disappointed about us keeping our incredible secret. Apparently, she's changed her mind.

If Maggie is okay with our teacherless class, then I am, too. Maggie's the most serious girl in school. She wears a sweatshirt that says HARVARD on the front. She always tells everyone that's where she is going to college, someday.

That's a long time from now, though.

To keep busy, I write. I write a story about a man who has nothing to do, so he sits on a chair all day long, day after day.

Cobwebs form between his fingers. His beard grows so long it hits the floor.

But still, he doesn't move. He has nothing better to do.

Eventually, demolition crews come to tear down the building where the man lives. The crews don't know the bored man lurks inside because no one has seen him in years. As the man hears the wrecking ball smash against the concrete walls and debris crumbles down around him, he stands. He wobbles, since he hasn't stood in a long time, and his muscles have grown saggy. But he staggers across the room and opens the front door. The light of day blinds him. He has forgotten how bright sunlight can be.

The crowd surrounding the building gasps. The man is as pale as a ghost and bone thin. At first, everyone thinks he's a zombie, but then they realize he's alive, and human.

"What have you been doing?" a woman in the crowd asks him.

"Nothing much," says the man.

But it's too late to stop the demolition. The wrecking ball swings again, and the walls collapse on top of the man. When the crowd finds him, buried in rubble, he's smiling.

"Why are you so happy?" a man asks him.

As the last flicker of life leaves his body, he replies, "Because for the first time in years, I'm not bored."

"Isn't it lunchtime?" asks Eli. He points to the classroom clock.

I look up from my paper. Lunch? Already? I rest my pencil on my desk and rise from my seat.

"But who will lead us to lunch?" asks Madelyn, light reflecting from her braces.

We all exchange confused gazes. No one knows. We always filed behind Ms. Bryce. But there is no Ms. Bryce here to file behind.

"I didn't bring a lunch," complains Cooper. "Maggie told Principal Klein that no one in our class is buying lunch today. So what am I supposed to eat?" Cooper looks like he's going to cry. No one has an answer for him.

And then I remember: I didn't bring my lunch, either. My stomach growls.

"Calm down," says Kyle. He frowns and grunts, "If we keep our mouths shut, everything will be fine."

"But I'm hungry!" whines Cooper.

"How about eating a smelly sock?" says Brian with a menacing hiss and a crack of his knuckles.

Cooper sniffles and chokes back one final sob.

There's a sliver of glass between the door and the wall, so I can see the hallway outside. Classes are streaming from their rooms to gather for their lunchroom walks. We need to join them in the hall. Teachers will notice if we're not in line and ready to go.

I expect Maggie to stand up and solve our problem. Or even Kyle. But they look as lost as the rest of the class, as if they are in a black tunnel and can't see the way out. No one takes charge.

So I clear my throat. "Uh, hey?" I say. A couple of kids glance over, but most ignore me. When you're usually invisible, it's hard to become visible again. I clear my throat again, this time louder. "Um, everyone?" My voice cracks. It's unaccustomed to being loud. It sounds weird to me.

My classmates notice me now. I hate the stares. I want to hide, but I can't hide after I've called everyone's attention to me. "Um . . . I think that we should assign a line leader to take us to lunch. And, um, so." I can feel my face blushing, but I keep going. "And, um, if you brought a lunch, how about sharing it with someone who didn't? Then, um, we can all eat something, you know?"

My face burns from the attention. It's probably bright red. But then a strange thing happens: No one yells at me to be quiet. No one shoves me or calls me nasty names for sharing lousy ideas.

Instead, my classmates nod their heads. They smile. They agree.

"Good idea," says Kyle.

Me! Eric Hill! I spoke up, and it was okay.

Those who brought lunches volunteer to share with kids who didn't. Emmy brought peanut butter and jelly and offers to split it with me.

I don't like jelly, especially not raspberry jelly, which is the flavor Emmy likes. But I don't say anything other than, "Sure. Thanks."

"Who wants to split my lunch?" asks Lizzie. "I brought ground lamb avocado balls. I made them myself."

No one says a word. I can't imagine anyone would want to eat lamb avocado balls.

I could write a horror story about lamb avocado balls.

"I will," says Adam.

Lizzie smiles broadly; the freckles on her cheeks stretch in size. Adam smiles back, but his face looks slightly greenish.

Adam's holding a sack lunch, but he drops it on the floor so Lizzie can't see that he brought his lunch today. I think of grabbing it so I don't have to share Emmy's sandwich, but Adam kicks it away and I'm guessing it's sort of ruined.

"Let's go!" announces Kyle.

No one moves. Everyone looks at me.

"Aren't you our line leader, Eric?" Jade asks, twirling her silky brown hair around her finger. She stares at me, waiting, her pale green eyes popping against her deep brown skin.

I hesitate. "Um. Me?" I've never been line leader before. I've never wanted to be. But someone has to, and how hard can it be? "Uh, sure." Adam and Lizzie get behind me, followed by Maggie and the brains. We walk out to the hall.

I lead. The others follow, single file.

It feels strange to be followed.

In the hallway, I stand next to the lockers, checking that everyone is lined up behind me. We look like we always do, except that we don't have a teacher in front.

In line, about fifteen kids back, Brian pushes Kyle. Kyle shoves Seth. Seth bangs into Madelyn. She gives a short yelp and backs into Gavin, stepping on one of his high-top sneakers.

Gavin, who's tall, toddles back and into Trevor. Trevor is short, so Gavin's elbow bumps into Trevor's chin. "Watch it," snaps Trevor, who pushes Gavin forward and into Madelyn, who then knocks into Seth.

Seth shoves her back into Gavin. It's like a nasty game of pinball.

Closer to me, Danny pushes Paige and giggles. Paige was holding a notebook, and it falls to the ground. She stumbles out of our line and into the hallway. "Stop it," she hisses to Danny, who is now pushing Jasmine.

"Leave me alone," complains Jasmine.

Danny snickers.

"What's going on here?" The booming voice of Principal Klein immediately halts the pushing and talking and snickering. Pushing and talking and snickering are against a hundred lunch-line rules. When we had rules.

Everyone stands straight, at attention. We're suddenly a well-trained army unit without an arm or leg out of line. We all stare ahead, at Ms. Bryce, if she were standing here.

"Where's your teacher?" asks Principal Klein. It sounds more like a demand than a question.

Our principal is a large man, and even though he wears orange cardigan sweaters, he's a little scary. Maybe it's the size of his hands. They are huge.

When he talks, I always stare at his hands.

I want to hide, but there's nowhere to run. In back of me, a few kids cough. None of us moves a muscle or says a word.

"I asked, where's Ms. Bryce?" our principal demands. His hands clench.

Again, no one says anything.

I answer softly, "She's in the bathroom."

I expect Principal Klein to accuse me of lying, jabbing his giant fingers into my chest, twisting my ear, and marching me to his office. Everyone will laugh at me.

Instead, Principal Klein says, "All right. But stop goofing off in the halls. You know better."

I can't believe we weren't busted. My heart is pounding as Mr. Klein heads back toward the front office. Once he's around the corner, I stumble forward and we're on our way down the hall.

Still, I'm so nervous, I can't breathe. I exhale only when I'm halfway down the hall.

When we get to the cafeteria, we all sit at our regular lunchroom table. Emmy gives me half of her peanut-butter-and-raspberry-jelly sandwich. I hoped there would be just a small dab of jelly over a thick spread of peanut butter. Instead, the sandwich is caked with gobs of jelly and just a small peanut-butter layer. Emmy also brought four cookies and gives me two of them. I think they are chocolate chip cookies, but I am extremely disappointed to discover they're oatmeal raisin.

I don't like raisins much, but I keep silent.

Around me, kids share their lunches without arguing. We can't misbehave or we'll be caught, so no one pushes anyone or starts a food fight, although there's some commotion at the other end, near the Big Goofs. Still, we've lasted more than twenty minutes with the rest of the fifth grade and no one has discovered our incredible secret.

But I just know this can't last for long.

9
KYLE

I reach across the lunchroom table and think:

Grab a cookie from Danny, a brownie from Trevor,
With no teachers around, it's the best lunchtime ever.

Maggie frowns at me. "Stop being a bully."

"Stop being annoying," I say, but I give Trevor back his brownie.

Just because I like dessert doesn't make me a bully, does it? She calls me a bully because I'm big, but I can't help it that I'm bigger than just about everyone else. Small kids are never called bullies.

After lunch we all head out to the playground for recess. The kickball gang runs off to play kickball. The four-square group gathers around the four-square grids. Monkey bar hangers hurry to hang out from their favorite perches.

No teachers or supervisors seem to notice that Ms. Bryce isn't sitting on the bench, like usual, watching us.

Most of the teachers stay indoors during recess, except Ms. Bryce always said she liked to keep an eye on us. But not now.

Now, this will be the best recess of all time.

Thunder rumbles overhead. It's a cloudy day, and it'll probably rain soon. For now, it's dry and anything goes.

I'm by the chain-link fence at the far end of the playground, between the swing sets and a few trees. Brian hurls a rock and nails a tree right in the center of the trunk. Seth does the same. I look down to find my own stone when something smashes into my shoulder. I feel a twinge of pain, although it quickly fades away. Brian laughs as a rock skips on the ground next to my feet.

"Whoops!" says Brian with a snort.

I bend down and scoop up a handful of small stones. Brian ducks behind a tree for shelter. I let a few of them fly, but they bounce off the bark. "Get out from there!" I yell, and fling another stone at the tree. It misses completely, and instead hits Seth's back.

"Watch it!" he hollers. He throws a stone back at me, but it smacks into a branch.

I look around. Normally, Ms. Bryce would be running over to yell at us by now. She saw everything, no matter where you stood or what you did. But not today. There is no Ms. Bryce anymore.

No one tells us to stop what we're doing. No one has noticed us.

Eli stands under one of the trees nearby. He huddles with Carl, a tall, lanky kid in Mr. Foley's fifth-grade class. The shadows from the leaves hide them. Their meeting reminds me of a scene from a spy movie.

They're whispering. Eli probably thinks he's out of earshot, but he's a loud whisperer.

"You're not going to believe what happened in our class yesterday," says Eli. "Ms. Bryce was our teacher, but then she—"

That's as far as he gets before Brian pops out from the tree he's been hiding behind, grabs Eli's arm, and yanks him backward. "What about your promise? Do you hate socks? Do you stink like a sock?" he hisses.

"I love socks!" shrieks Eli. "I mean, I love regular socks, not smelly socks. I'm not really sure if I understand the whole smelly sock thing, actually, but whatever it is, I don't like it."

"Oh, I think you hate socks, but you love smelly ones," says Brian, looking as confused as Eli. Then he sniffs the air and says, "I think we'll call you Smelly Sock Eli." Brian is about twice Eli's size, and he keeps his hand clutched on the smaller kid's arm, squeezing tightly.

"What about you?" Brian snarls to Carl, towering over him.

"I don't smell like anything or think about socks or whatever, dude," he says. He holds his hands up and steps away.

I laugh because the whole thing is pretty ridiculous to

watch. But then I think of Maggie's words at lunch. She called me a bully, but I'm not. At least I don't think I am. I stride over to Brian and clap my hand on his back. I know it's fun to pick on smaller kids, but I suppose they can't help being smaller.

"Leave him alone. He won't squeal, right?" I say. "Eli doesn't smell like a sock."

Brian maintains his grip on Eli, sniffing the air. "I smell something."

"That's just your own stinky breath," I say, giving Brian a friendly punch on the arm.

Brian releases Eli's arm. "What's wrong with my breath?"

I smile. "I'm just kidding." I'm probably the only one who can tease Brian without fearing for his life. "Come on. Let's throw rocks at Seth."

As Brian and I step away, Eli shakes his head, but his legs are shaking just as much. He looks as if he's escaped a car wreck, unharmed. I hear Carl ask him, "What was that about, dude?"

"Nothing," says Eli.

It seems to me that when people say something is "nothing," it usually is a pretty big something.

Brian and I bend over to collect stones. So does Seth. We all pick trees to duck behind. But I only have time to throw a couple of rocks, missing badly each time, when the school bell rings, announcing the end of recess.

Teachers stand near the main door waiting for their students to gather. Kids run to get in line, single file, waiting to be escorted back to their rooms.

The three of us drop our rocks and start heading toward the school to go inside and get in line, too.

"Where are we going?" I ask.

We stop.

There is no teacher to line us up. No one tells us to go back to class.

There are no recess rules for us.

As the playground empties, we freeze by the four-square grids. Most of our class gathers around us.

"What do we do now?" asks Danny.

"Shouldn't we go inside?" asks Jasmine.

"Why?" asks Brian. He grabs a ball that's rolled away from the finished kickball game. He picks it up and dribbles it twice. "Let's have a ball out here," he says, laughing, and then bounces the ball off Danny's head.

He picks up the ball and gets ready to throw it again when Mrs. Crawford strolls up to our group, her lips pinched. Our group circle opens up to let her in. "Why aren't you lining up?" she demands.

Her class waits by the school entrance in an orderly and noiseless row.

Mrs. Crawford is one of the other fifth-grade teachers. She's not as old as Ms. Bryce, but she's not too far behind.

I groan, but I don't think she hears me. I'm still holding a rock, so I drop it.

No one says a word. Mrs. Crawford rests her hands on her hips, waiting for an answer. Her eyes twitch. "Where is Ms. Bryce?" she asks, scanning the playground.

She looks at me, and I meet her gaze. I feel like a deer in headlights. I open my mouth, but no words come out.

There's a long silence.

"I asked, where is Ms. Bryce?" she repeats.

"She's in the bathroom," says Eric, who I didn't notice standing next to me.

It's easy not to notice Eric.

"Well, you should be lining up," says Mrs. Crawford.

"Right," says Eric. "Ms. Bryce, um, said she'd be back in a minute and told us to wait for her. Do you want us to, uh, line up anyway?"

Mrs. Crawford shakes her head. "No, that's okay. Follow her instructions."

"Because, um, we totally could," Eric suggests.

"No, no. You're fine," says Mrs. Crawford, heading back to her class. Soon, she is escorting them inside the school building.

A crack of thunder rumbles from above. The clouds overhead us are black. All the classes are inside, except ours. We stand together, but then Brian throws his ball at Danny's head again.

"Hey!" yelps Danny.

I laugh.

Yow. Yow. Yow.

Recess might just last forever!

Brian picks up the ball again, and everyone runs away. A game of ball tag quickly erupts between the boys.

I shove Gavin, even though I don't have the ball, and laugh again.

No one is outside telling me not to shove anyone.

A squeak of laughter erupts from a group of girls near us, and Jasmine appears to be close to tears. Are the other girls being mean to her?

No one is outside telling us to act nice.

But then more thunder grumbles in the sky. Another roar of thunder booms, and a few drops of rain follow.

The few drops quickly turn into many drops. Soon, we're all rushing inside the school as water soaks our clothes and hair.

So much for extended outside recess. I suppose we'll just need to continue our permanent *indoor* recess now.

10

MAGGIE

Goofing off continues in class today. I'd hoped that the longer pre-rain recess time today would tire some of my rowdier classmates, but I think it's only made them rowdier.

I once read that there are more than one hundred million cells in the human brain. Most of my classmates are using about five.

For most of the morning, I searched diligently through Ms. Bryce's work sheets. Now, I pick up where I left off. My plan takes shape, as surely as two negatives form a positive when multiplied together.

An eraser collides against my arm. "Sorry!" says Brian with a snicker. He's not sorry, though, not in the least. Those Neanderthals are never sorry.

I'm sitting at the teacher's desk. Why not? If I am going to whip this class into learning shape, where else would I sit? So when the phone rings, I pick it up before the first ring ends.

My desk. My phone. My class.

"May I help you?" I ask. No more mousy voice for me.

"Is this Ms. Bryce?" Principal Klein asks.

"Who else would it be?" I say, ducking the question.

"Is everything okay?"

I cough. I take a deep breath. I remind myself that I am Maggie Cranberry, and I have every right to answer this phone.

We need to keep our secret so I can take charge.

That single thought fires my millions of brain cells.

"Of course," I say. "Why would you think everything wasn't perfectly satisfactory?"

"No one has been sent to detention all day," he says. "Or yesterday afternoon, for that matter. And, well, that's not like your class. So you can see why I'm concerned."

Right. Our class gets in trouble a lot.

I feel myself breaking out in a sweat. I bite my lip.

Breathe. I can handle this. Go!

"My students have been behaving today," I reply. "Especially that Maggie Cranberry. Now that's a girl who is going places."

"Um. Are you feeling well? You don't sound like yourself."

"I've never been better!" Maybe I was laying it on too thick. After all, I'm supposed to be Ms. Bryce, and Ms. Bryce would never rave about her students. When criminals rob banks, they always get tripped up on small details. They leave a fingerprint. They brag to someone about what they did.

They drop their wallets at the crime scene. Not that we're robbing a bank, and not that we're criminals. But the analogy feels appropriate.

"Funny that you called," I say. "I was just sending someone to your office this very moment."

"Good. I mean, not good. I'm sorry your class is misbehaving. But I'm glad everything is normal."

"Of course. Why wouldn't things be normal? Everything here is exemplary," I say, with maybe too much energy. My voice cracks.

I hang up the phone, but my hand trembles. If I'm going to lead this class, I'll need to be more careful. I need to remember that I'm not taking charge for *me* but for everyone in Class 507. This is for their educations, for their futures, and for their millions of unused brain cells.

And my getting into Harvard is just a little extra gravy on the mashed potatoes of excellence.

But we need to send someone to detention *now*.

Eyeing Brian, Kyle, and Seth hurling erasers, I know any one of those troublemakers would be the perfect candidate to march down the hall. But they wouldn't listen. If I ordered one of them to the principal's office, they would probably just throw an eraser at me.

No, I need everyone in class to agree with me. I need a consensus, a plurality, a democracy-voting-majority-true-blue American election.

I stand up and pound a stapler on the desk, like a judge slams a gavel. Everyone stops what they are doing and looks at me, as I intended. "We need to send someone to the principal's office," I announce. The class groans. "To keep up appearances. Principal Klein is getting suspicious since no one has gotten into any trouble today. Who wants to go?"

No one raises a hand, but that's not surprising. Blockheads never like to face the consequences of their blockheaded-ness.

"Then I'll just pick someone," I say.

Trevor whispers to Gavin, "There goes Miss Bossy, *again*." I glare at him, daring him to say something else about me, but he shrinks in his seat.

I am not bossy. I'm a leader. There's a big difference.

"Why don't we draw straws?" suggests Eric. "Maybe, um, who pulls the shortest straw goes to detention?"

Drawing straws. That's actually a good idea. Maybe that small, quiet kid Eric is less of a blockhead than some of the others.

Ryan looks through the filing cabinet of supplies against the far wall, where it stands under the picture of the most populous North American birds. (I have them memorized. They include blue jays, robins, cardinals, geese, and goldfinches.) There are pencils and markers and tape and tissue papers inside the cabinet but apparently "no straws," she reports, and then does a ballet spin because, well, because Ryan always spins.

"We can use pencils," Eric suggests.

That's another good idea from him.

Ryan spins up to the desk, bringing two boxes of pencils with her. I count out twenty pencils, one for every student in class except me—as the self-appointed and decidedly non-bossy leader of this class, I can't be sent to detention.

I break one pencil in half and put it, along with the nineteen unbroken pencils, in my fist. No one can see which is the shortened, broken one.

The kids in class walk up and grab a pencil, one at a time. Brian snags the very last one. I'm disappointed to see it isn't the short pencil.

"Who has it?" I ask.

"Not me," says Brian.

"Not me," says Trevor.

"I've got it," says Adam, holding up his stub for us all to see. He sinks his shoulders. "I better get going to the principal's office, I guess."

That figures. Adam always gets detention.

11

SAMANTHA

On Wednesday, breakfast waits for me on our dining room table, like it's supposed to. As I take my usual chair, I'm excited about school today. I can't remember being this excited about anything.

At least, I can't remember being this excited about anything that doesn't include shoes.

On the table, my utensils glisten. I smooth a bump from my hair, using the reflection from my spoon for guidance. I put a cloth napkin on my lap.

Everything is perfect.

Wait. It's not.

Because when I look down at the plate in front of me, my stomach ties itself into a big knot. The yolk dribbles into the egg whites, and the egg whites run into the whole-wheat toast. The crusts on my toast have been sliced off, *mostly*. But on one edge, parts of the terrible-tasting, too-hard brown bread exterior remain.

Ugh.

I lift my fork, but I don't eat. I stare.

"Eat up, Sam. Eggs are good for you," says my aunt Karen. She came to stay with us for a few weeks when I was in kindergarten, and she never left. Fortunately. Because Aunt Karen is a fabulous chef most of the time and Mom does *not* cook, thank you very much. But today my aunt's eggs over easy are making me uneasy.

She smiles, but I return her grin with an icy frown.

Daddy always tells me that the squeaky wheel gets the grease. Not that I want to be greased! But constructive criticism is important. I learned that lesson from Ms. Bryce, too. She loved to criticize.

It may be the only thing I learned from her.

"The eggs are too runny," I say.

"Oh, they're fine," says Aunt Karen. She stands over me. She's a big woman, with wide shoulders and thick arms. She shakes her head at me, as if I'm at fault here, but I meet her stare.

Uncooked eggs can make you sick, and crusts are just sickening.

You know what? They should bake bread without crusts. I'll talk to Daddy about that. He'll be impressed by my business savvy. He could make a fortune, not that he needs another one.

"Oh, there you are, sweetheart." Mom whirls into the

kitchen like a tornado. She's a blur of motion, her arms waving, and my napkin flutters off my lap from the breeze that blows behind her. She's wearing a short white tennis skirt. The bracelets on her gesturing arms clang together, gold against gold against silver.

She's like a tornado-whirling wind chime.

A tennis racket sticks out of the gym bag strapped across her shoulder.

"Eggs?" asks Aunt Karen, stepping back to the stove and lifting the runny goop from the frying pan.

Aunt Karen starts to slide the eggs to a shiny clean plate, but Mom waves her off. "Aren't you a dear? But I can't, I'm late! I'm meeting the girls for our Wednesday morning tennis match, and then I'm off to the spa. Busy, busy!" She bends down and kisses the air next to my cheek, and I kiss her cheek air back. With a jingling wave, the tornado hurries into the living room and presses the button for the elevator.

We have our own elevator, of course. Last year it broke for a whole week, and I had to ride the *service* elevator. They call it that because *service* people use it, like maintenance people and garbage collectors, and the elevator smells awful. Mom always keeps an air freshener in ours. It was a simply terrible week.

"What about your breakfast?" Aunt Karen asks as I bring my plate to the sink, but I'm already turning around and following Mom's path.

"No time, I gotta go! See you later!" I call behind me. I grab my fur-collared jacket and my backpack, and I hop into the elevator right before it closes.

Mom puts on lipstick, staring into her small cosmetics mirror. I slide my arms into my jacket sleeves. We ride down in silence until Mom twists her lipstick back into the tube. She asks, "So. How's school?"

I know I shouldn't say anything about, well, *you know*. We all promised. But I'm excited to tell *someone*. The secret has been building for two days. I feel like I'm about to burst. I almost told Aunt Karen yesterday. I really wanted to when she was kissing me good-night (no air kisses from her!) but caught myself at the last moment.

"You'll never guess what happened on Monday," I blurt out to Mom. "The most amazing, fantastic, and surprising thing. Our teacher, Ms.—"

The elevator door opens and Mom rushes out. "I'm sorry, darling. I must run. Have a great day!" The tornado leaves me behind in its wake.

"But—" I stand in the elevator by myself, feeling sort of foolish with my mouth open in the middle of an unfinished sentence. I take a breath and step into the building lobby.

The doors close behind me with a melodic TING!

As I walk across the floor, my dark green glossy leather boots clip-clop on the marble.

Up ahead, George holds the heavy glass door open for me. As I walk by, he tips his doorman's cap and tilts his head in a semi-bow. "Have a wonderful day, Miss Samantha," he says.

"You too," I call back.

I smile. I love it when adults call me *Miss*.

I turn left at the sidewalk to head to school. Right next to our building is an old folks' home. Daddy calls it a "retirement community," but that's just a longer name for a home for old folks.

Sitting in a lawn chair on the grass, near the edge of the sidewalk of the Old Buzzards' Building (there! I called it something else!), sits Mr. Wolcott. He's wearing a brown three-piece suit that was probably fashionable in 1940-something and a striped tie that's as wide as his neck. I think it's called an *ascot*. He wears the same suit and sits on the same chair every day, rain or shine, although if it rains he holds an umbrella.

"How are you on this most sunny of days, Franny?" he booms to me, with a theatrical wave of his hand. He is so loud that two or three people walking near us turn to look, thinking something is wrong.

But it's just Mr. Wolcott.

"My name is Samantha, Mr. Wolcott." I've told him this, oh, five thousand times.

"Of course, of course. But you look like my Franny—Franny Bree, siren of the stage. The beauty of Broadway. Have I told you that before?"

"Every day," I say with a sigh.

"She was just about your age when she first appeared in the theater. I remember the day well. She was resplendent. A nightingale of nimbleness! Oh, I was just an understudy then—a piece of lint on her lace gown hem. I was in love with Franny even then. Who was not? A vision, she was! But summer's lease hath all too short a date."

"I really need to get to school," I say, hurrying off before he can start quoting more things to me. He's harmless, but if you linger too long, he'll just talk and talk and quote stuff and make you late for wherever you're going.

And I don't want to be late for school. Not today. Anything could happen today.

And I bet anything *will* happen.

As I dash off, I'm weighted down by my backpack. It's extra heavy because I stuffed a bunch of my fashion magazines inside it last night. I plan to share some with Giovanna.

I'm carrying the emerald-green backpack today. It exactly matches the shade of my boots. No one else matches their backpacks with their shoes, which, if you ask me, is a big mistake.

I spin and fluff my hair. I could be the star of the stage, just like Franny What's-Her-Name that Mr. Wolcott is always talking about. Why not? I could star in my own fashion magazine, too.

Maybe I'll ask Daddy to buy one for me.

Not a fashion magazine issue, but the entire corporate headquarters.

As I turn the corner, I think about breakfast and sort of feel bad for complaining about it. Maybe I should have tried the eggs.

But then again, if I'm hungry, I can always just eat some of my lunch in class. I know Ms. Bryce had rules about that sort of thing.

But not anymore.

12
MAGGIE

Before school, I ignore my breakfast bagel while I scan through the thick book that's open on my kitchen table. The book details the long history of Harvard University. I had requested it at our library, so the other week when I received the email informing me the book was finally available, I made Mom drive me to pick it up immediately.

I'm reading the book start to finish, of course. Harvard was founded in 1636, so there is a lot to read.

But getting into Harvard is not easy, even with a history of parents and relatives graduating from it. I still need to earn my spot. Sure, my friends are always telling me that I shouldn't worry about college yet.

But if not now, when?

My father won a national science contest when he was only twelve years old. I'll turn twelve soon enough. Okay, maybe not that soon. But really, now *is* the time to worry about my future.

Teaching a fifth-grade class after my teacher quits will look very impressive. No one else in my family ever did that. It's crucial to have life experiences that make your college application stand out from the other ten thousand rolling across the desk.

Did you know Harvard gets more than 30,000 applications a year and only accepts about 2,000 of them?

That means they have (approximately) 28,000 denied applicants a year. That's (approximately) 28,000 annual failures.

Winter break starts in a couple of weeks, and I'm electrified, thrilled, and aflutter. Mom, Dad, and I are going to visit Harvard. This will be my first time there. I want to see everything.

Mom says we should go to Disneyland or something instead. She says I'll be bored. On the other hand, Dad says that the present is a present that needs to be unwrapped and used to invest in tomorrow. I couldn't agree more.

But the present means *today* and not eleven days from now. Today is the day I start Operation Anti-Blockhead. I just hope everyone appreciates how I'm going to help them learn and unwrap each of their gift-wrapped presents.

Whipping my classmates into shape shouldn't be a problem. Teaching is a snap. If Ms. Bryce could do it, then I can, too.

"Ready for school?" Mom asks.

"Am I ever," I reply, strolling past Mom and to our garage.

Last year, the school bus had a flat tire and we arrived thirty minutes late. *Never again*, I said. School is too important. I like to ride my bike when I can, but it's too cold to ride it now. So Mom drives me every morning. I always insist we leave early. That way I'm the first one to arrive in class.

I'll have the room to myself for thirty minutes. I have plenty to do.

Ten minutes later we pull up (before many of the teachers!), Mom kisses me, and I hurry to class. Once inside, I sit at the teacher's desk that is now *my* desk. I make a long list of responsibilities that need to be assigned.

I've also started searching through Ms. Bryce's papers. Since she's been a teacher for just about forever, she has lots and lots of papers. I'll be adding my own touches to them, of course. The assignments must be challenging so my classmates rise from the depths of mediocrity and soar on the wings of academic alacrity!

That means they'll be excited, fired up, and ready to learn.

Time flies and soon the warning bell rings in the hall, signaling four minutes and fifty-three seconds until class starts. (The bell is supposed to signal five minutes until class starts, but the timer is fast. I've clocked it against my watch.) Students pile in. Brian enters and immediately hurls an eraser at Kyle. Cooper lugs a big stack of comic books. Trevor flips a football back and forth in his hands. He tosses it to Gavin, who spikes it on the ground and then yells, "Touchdown!" I shake my head. Those boys are all 100 percent blockheads.

I wait until the bell rings, and then I stand up, pounding my stapler on my desk. It takes three hits before everyone stops their mindless yapping and looks at me. "Thank you," I say. "I understand fun and games is, um, fun. But we can't spend every day doing nothing but playing."

"Why not?" asks Seth, way in the back of the room. Brian nods. So do Danny and Jasmine.

"There goes Miss Bossy again," Trevor whispers to Gavin. I stiffen and try to brush off his comment.

"I would much rather goof off, too," I say, my voice rolling with false enthusiasm. The art of persuasive communication is tricky. I've read that if you sympathize with your audience, they'll listen to you more. So I continue with my most caring voice, even if I don't believe a word of what I'm saying.

After all, I *am* caring. I am a lot more caring than I am bossy, anyway.

"Who wouldn't rather play?" I continue. I clear my throat. "But our parents will grow suspicious if we don't have homework and take tests."

Brian hurls an eraser at me, but it misses and strikes the wall, bouncing harmlessly off the whiteboard. I don't flinch. Leaders never flinch.

"I don't want homework!" Brian complains.

"Neither do I," I say, although I *do* want homework. I mean, I want to *give* homework. "But it is only work if a teacher assigns it to you. If we assign it to ourselves, then it's kind of like playing."

" 'If we assign it to ourselves, then it's kind of like playing,' " says Brian. He repeats my words using an odd, high-pitched voice that I think is supposed to mimic mine, but sounds nothing like me. He's way too whiny. I don't whine. Bossy people might whine, but leaders lead.

I ignore Brian's intended mockery. "Learning isn't work if you learn on your own."

" 'Learning isn't work—' " begins Brian in his squeaky voice.

"Knock it off," says Kyle. "She has a point."

I raise an eyebrow. I never would have thought Kyle Anderson, of all people in the world, would listen to me.

I'll need to reevaluate his 100 percent blockheadedness. Perhaps it's only 98 percent block.

I flash him a grateful smile.

Brian sits down, but he looks annoyed.

"Our parents asked why we didn't have any homework last night," Danny says, looking at his twin sister, Jasmine. "We always have homework."

"Mine asked me the same thing," says Jade with a big frown.

"Mine too," Madelyn adds. "And so did my orthodontist." She points to her braces.

"When my parents asked why I didn't have homework, I panicked and told them I had a huge test today," whimpers Gavin. "If I don't bring home a graded test soon, they'll wonder what's going on."

More kids groan. Others mention similar concerns. Emmy's parents almost emailed the teacher yesterday, asking if she'd left her homework at school.

I lean back, letting the class talk. They are convincing themselves of the importance of homework, which only makes my job easier.

"But we don't have a teacher," Danny says. "So how are we going to have tests?"

Kids continue to moan. They argue. They fear that even one more day without homework will trigger phone calls, school visits, and general chaos.

I smirk to myself.

"Only smelly sock haters want a teacher," growls Brian. "Or smelly sock lovers, or whatever."

This conversation has gone on long enough. I need to resume order. I slap the stapler against the desk twice. A few kids continue to complain. I stand behind my desk, stapler in hand, ready to bang it down again. But Kyle barks, "Quiet!" and the entire class silences. Kyle's blockhead percentage lowers even more. Everyone looks at me.

"Thank you," I say. "I've given this a lot of thought. I have a solution." I pause so the class eagerly awaits my next words. I hold my tongue. The anticipation mounts. A few kids lean forward.

"Someone has to make a sacrifice for the good of the class," I continue, my chin high. Heroic. Heroes always have jutted chins. "And that someone will be me. I don't *want* to make this tiresome, laboring sacrifice, believe me." I keep my smile from bursting out. Instead, I keep the very deep and sincere expression that I am faking on my face. "But I will. I will assign and grade homework. I will give tests. I, *of course*, would much rather play games. But I will take responsibility for keeping us out of trouble." I give a deep, loud sigh and frown.

"You would do that for us?" asks Lacey.

"You're so noble!" exclaims Paige.

I bite my lip to keep my smile from spreading too much. I remind myself that I'm not supposed to be enjoying this. I am making a sacrifice, even if it will help me, too.

"So what happens now?" asks Emmy.

I lift a piece of paper from the desk. I clear my throat. "First of all, we need to have a little discipline. We can't be running outside taking extra recess, for example. I've assigned jobs. If we band together, then no one will discover our secret. Then, we'll have the best year ever. Are you with me?"

The class cheers. Even Brian raises his fist. Kyle pounds his desk in agreement. Trevor and Gavin smile, too.

Convincing the class is easy.

Just like being a teacher is easy.

I go through my list with the class. Emmy will take attendance and lunch count every day. Eli will bring it to the office. Kyle will feed Soda, the room hamster. Madelyn will be our line leader for lunch. And so on.

I will grade, assign, lead the class, and hold the pencils for our daily detention drawing, which we should do every day, with today's drawing now. Principal Klein will expect a detention note every day, and we shall not disappoint him.

The entire class gathers around me, and they each grab one of the twenty pencils clutched in my fists. "Who has the stub?" I ask.

"Not me!" says Brian.

"Not me!" says Trevor.

Adam raises his hand and groans. "I do."

As Adam frowns, I pass out work sheets to the class. I've added extra questions to them, so they are more challenging. "And we'll have a test Friday," I say.

No one complains. Gavin says, "Thanks for the homework."

"My pleasure," I respond.

After I've passed out the assignments, I sit back at my

desk. Lacey and Paige approach me. "We can help," Lacey suggests.

"It's really a one-person job," I insist. "But thanks, anyway."

"Maybe we can prepare some work sheets?" asks Lacey.

"Or come up with test questions?" suggests Paige.

"No, no. I will do it all myself," I say. This will be a piece of cake.

I am Maggie Cranberry, and my future is looking so bright I wish I had worn sunglasses to school.

13
ERIC

It's quiet in the house. Too quiet. When I think of quiet things, I think of ghosts, and when I think of ghosts, I get nervous.

I suppose there are nice ghosts and mean ghosts, just like there are nice people and mean people. But you never know which sort of ghost you'll get, and once you get ghosts, there's nothing much you can do about them. You're haunted, and that's that.

But there aren't ghosts here, not really. At least I hope not. It's noisy in class, and I guess I've just gotten used to the continual screaming. I wish I could put on the TV—the sound would make the room feel less scary—but Mom doesn't let me watch television on school days.

Maggie gave us more homework than Ms. Bryce ever did, and Ms. Bryce gave us a lot. I have a pile of math work sheets, reading logs, and more.

Maggie says it's not really homework since we're assigning it ourselves, but it sure feels like homework to me.

Most of these sheets appear to be from Ms. Bryce's files, but I think Maggie created a few on her own. There is a work sheet on "Why Homework Is Awesome!" and I'm pretty sure that's a Maggie original.

Maggie explained that if she gave us *more* homework than usual, no one would suspect we didn't have a teacher. I guess that makes sense, sort of. I just wish she didn't look so happy about assigning it. As Maggie handed out new work sheets, her face was one giant grin. She kept insisting she was making a big sacrifice creating homework.

I'm not sure if Maggie really felt she was making much of a sacrifice at all.

We thought not having a teacher would mean less work, but it sure seems like we have a lot more.

I sit at the kitchen table with my homework, a glass of milk, and a plate of saltine crackers. I have a napkin, too. My mom doesn't like me to make crumbs.

I sip my milk and then take out a new yellow pencil, freshly sharpened, and get to work. I don't want to be the only one in class who doesn't complete the assignments.

I don't want to stand out.

But instead, I write a story in my notebook.

My story is about a kid who always stands out. I call him Cire, because that's Eric spelled backward and he's the opposite of me. He wears bright orange shirts to school, always talks as loudly as he can, and raises his hand for every question in class, even when he doesn't know the answers. Often, he blurts out answers without even being picked.

Everyone hates him.

One day someone decides to teach him a lesson. Cire loves gum. He's always chewing it. So someone puts a pack of gum in his locker, forcing it through the slats. When Cire opens his locker, he just assumes the pack of gum is his.

He puts a stick in his mouth. Cire doesn't know the gum has been secretly filled with superglue.

As soon as class starts, their teacher, Mrs. Brick, asks a question. Cire's arm shoots straight up. Before the teacher can even call on him, he starts to speak.

But his mouth is superglued shut. Although Cire tries to speak, he can't open his lips.

Sweat forms on his forehead. Cire mumbles, "Mmmm . . . mmmmm," but that's all he can say.

"I don't find this funny at all," says the teacher.

"Mmmmm . . ."

Finally, the teacher points to the door. "If you insist on muttering nonsense, then you can go to the principal's office right now."

Cire stands up, still mumbling. The teacher frowns at him. "I hope you learn your lesson."

Mrs. Brick smiles to herself. She's happy that she can now

choose other kids without Cire always interrupting. As he leaves the room, Mrs. Brick pats the outside of her pants pocket, where she can feel the special pack of superglue-spiked gum she brought to school that day, resting inside.

It's not one of my better stories. I am about to rip it out of the book and throw it away when I notice a shadow hovering over my page. My mom stands over me. "What are you doing?"

"I was about to do homework," I explain, quickly flipping to a blank page and lifting a work sheet. I don't show Mom any of my stories. She'd just tell me they're a waste of time.

"Do we write on the table without a place mat?" she asks with a frown. It's not really a question. "You could get pencil marks on the wood."

Our yellow vinyl place mats are next to me, stacked neatly on top of one another. I remove the top one and slide it under my notebook. "Sorry."

"And what do we say about putting coasters under glasses?" she asks. Again, it's a question but not a question.

I don't see a coaster, so I put my glass on the copy of *Hamlet* that I'm still reading.

I'm not really reading it. I'm agonizing over reading it.

"Sorry, again," I mumble quietly.

"Don't mumble," says Mom. "You sound like your mouth is glued shut."

"I said I'm sorry," I say again, louder and more clearly.

"Fine," she says, satisfied. "Now give me a kiss."

She bends over so that her cheek is within range of my mouth. I give her a quick peck.

She straightens up, but then she shakes her head at me. "Don't slouch, either. It's bad for your back."

I sit up straighter.

"That's better. I love you." Mom leaves the room, and once she's out the door I begin writing another story. This one is about a mom who always lets her son make messes at the kitchen table and sit however he wants to sit.

It's a boring story, but it makes me smile.

14

KYLE

As I sit down in class, I unzip my backpack and remove my homework that's not really homework.

I did it last night, and I have no teacher.

Yow. Yow. Yow.

Who would have imagined *that*?

Yesterday, when Maggie suggested we do homework, I thought it was a good idea, at first.

I figured that if I did lots of homework, I could prove to Mom that I'm good for something.

But I didn't even get to show her my work because she sent me to my room after I came home two hours late.

Mom had asked me to come straight home from school so I could watch the twins and Marley while she ran some errands. But I forgot and played tag football with Brian and the guys.

Since I was banished to my room, I couldn't watch TV or anything. Instead I did my homework that's not really homework.

The assignment was *not* easy, either. I reread a chapter of my math textbook so I could complete some of the more difficult questions on one of the work sheets. It turns out I had two of the formulas backward, and one I completely misunderstood. It took a while, but I finished all of the questions, and I think I got them all right.

I felt proud to finish the work.

But Mom was too busy to look at it. And then I remembered that we didn't have a teacher. That sucked most of that pride out the window.

Still, maybe I'm better at schoolwork than I've always thought. Maybe, just maybe, I could be a good student if I just tried my hardest and didn't give up so easily.

Which is a strange thing to think, right?

Before I went to bed, I asked Mom about her promotion. She said she was still thinking about it.

"What's to think about?" I asked.

"It would mean more time at the office," she said. "Who would take care of all of you?"

"I could help."

She just smiled, shrugged, and kissed me good-night.

I don't think she trusts me to take care of anything. But she's wrong. I can help, just like I can do my homework that isn't homework.

I can become a brand-new Kyle. I know it. I'll show Mom, too. I'm just not sure how.

In class, I flip the eraser between my fingers and look at Brian. I balance the pink rubber rectangle on my fingertips.

The brand-new Kyle doesn't throw erasers.

I bury it in my hand. I can't spend *every* day whipping erasers at people, can I?

THUNK!

An eraser bounces off the side of my head. Brian laughs. "Head shot! Two points!"

I tell the voice inside my head, the one that's been whispering that I shouldn't be such a goofball, to *go away*!

Because I can't let a head shot go unanswered, can I?

I hurl my eraser at Brian, where it smacks his ear.

"Ear shot! Three points!" I declare.

In Eraser Wars, hitting an ear is worth three points. Hitting the head is worth two points, striking the body is worth just one point, and a nose shot is worth a whopping four points.

Colds and allergies can hurt your nose,

But they don't compare to eraser nose blows.

That's when I notice Brian holding an entire handful of erasers.

He must have brought them from home.

Uh-oh.

Seth and I duck under our desks as erasers whiz around us like artillery fire. BING! BAM! POW! They strike the desk and the floor and the chair.

"Will you guys just knock it off?" Maggie complains from the front of the room, standing up.

Brian whips an eraser at Maggie, but it misses.

"Stop being so bossy!" Brian yells.

"I'm not bossy," says Maggie, but softly, her voice cracking, and she sits down.

"Has anyone noticed the smell is almost gone?" asks Jasmine.

I peek back up from under the desk. Brian isn't holding any more erasers. I stand up and sniff.

I was so used to the terrible odors from the vinegar volcano that I forgot about them. I guess you can get used to just about anything.

Even doing homework, maybe.

But Jasmine is right. The vinegar smell still lingers in the room, but faintly. I have to take a good long sniff to notice it at all.

"What's going to keep other teachers away now?" asks Madelyn.

Principal Klein could walk in, and then what? He would open the door and get smashed on the forehead with an eraser.

We'd be hauled away to detention for a year.

"They can't find out," moans Maggie. "We can't have a teacher *yet*!"

I thought Maggie *wanted* a teacher.

"We'll probably be given twice as much homework," groans Danny, although Maggie gave us plenty. Danny wears these tight dreadlocks, and he pulls them as he fidgets. Jasmine wears her hair the same way. She pulls hers, too. It must be a twin thing.

"They'll probably give us the meanest teacher ever," says Emmy. "Maybe we'll get Ms. Bryce's evil clone."

"We are going to be in so much trouble," Danny moans.

Adam spits on his desk and rubs it with his shirtsleeve. His desk is covered in doodles and tiny hearts, and his sleeve wipes only some of the marks off. It smudges others. I guess he's trying to erase the evidence of his doodles before we're discovered, so he can avoid detention.

Lizzie wipes her desk, too. It's also covered in tiny hearts.

"We could always, um, post a lookout," says Eric.

Adam and Lizzie stop rubbing.

"What do you mean?" I ask.

Eric's a small kid, and his voice is small. We have to be quiet to hear him. "Well, see, um, with a lookout we can take turns standing outside the door." Eric looks down, as if embarrassed to talk. "When a teacher comes by, um, the lookout can knock two times on the door. One, two. Then we can quickly stop whatever we're doing, right? And we can, uh, pretend to be working, maybe."

"But won't the teacher wonder why we're standing in the hallway?" asks Lacey.

Eric nods. Still casting his eyes to the floor, he says, "We'll just say our teacher is giving us a time-out. That's the sort of thing Ms. Bryce would do, right?"

It *is* something she would do.

Yow. Yow. Yow. A lookout. That's a fantastic idea.

Everyone nods their heads.

"We should take turns," Paige suggests. "How about we do it alphabetically?"

That seems fair. My eyes go to the far wall, where our class list is taped. The first name, on the very top of the list, is Kyle Anderson.

Me.

"I'll go out in a minute," I say. Because I just noticed a whole bunch of erasers by my feet, left from where Brian threw them earlier.

I wink at Seth, who notices all the erasers on the floor, too. Brian is out of ammunition. And we're not.

Let Eraser War revenge begin!

I've added nine more points to my total when there's a knock on the door. Everyone in class stops whatever they are doing and freezes.

I was supposed to be the lookout, wasn't I?

My arm is cocked and about to zip my final eraser, but I

lower my hand. My eyes dart to the door. It swings open and Principal Klein walks in.

Gavin and Trevor stop playing tic-tac-toe on the whiteboard and quickly try to erase it. Maggie looks up from where she's sitting on the teacher's chair. Ryan stands on her desk, where I think she was spinning.

"What's going on?" Principal Klein demands. "Where is your teacher?" He glares at us, his big hands tensed.

It's so quiet you could hear a pencil drop. We all look at one another, afraid to move, and even more afraid to speak.

Trouble is about to fall on us like a terrible avalanche.

After what feels like forever, that quiet kid Eric clears his throat and speaks up again. "Ms. Bryce is in the bathroom."

Principal Klein frowns. He looks at Ryan, still standing on a desk. "And what do you think you're doing, young lady?"

"Um," she mutters.

Eric clears this throat again. "We're doing an, um, experiment with heat. Heat rises, right? So we're, uh, measuring the temperature at different heights in the room. Maggie is getting thermometers. And Gavin and Trevor are recording our findings."

Good one. Maybe I should notice Eric more. It's easy to forget he's here.

I look at Eric and then at our principal, who is gazing around the room. No one breathes. But then Principal Klein nods. "Okay then. Good work. Carry on. But keep it down. Some of the other classes say you're being loud."

And he leaves. Just like that.

All of us, everyone in class, lets loose a unified deep breath of relief. That was way close.

A bunch of my classmates now stare at me. Some of them frown.

"I thought you were supposed to be the lookout," says Maggie.

"Yeah, but—" I start to say.

"We should have known you'd mess up," says Lacey. "You're not good for anything."

I cringe at those words. I stomp my foot. I think about my mom and her promotion and the new Kyle I'm going to be. The new Kyle who I'm supposed to be.

"I'm going. Are you happy?" I bark.

As I cross the room, stares follow me. I glare right back. I knock off Trevor's baseball cap, just because. I'm relieved when I step out into the hallway and away from the glares. I loudly bang the door behind me.

It pops back open, so I kick it closed again.

BANG!

But . . . now what?

I shift to my right foot, and then to my left. I hop. I stare at the door.

I'm bored.

I sit on the floor. It's boring on the floor, too.

I hear kids laughing from inside our classroom. This isn't fair. I stand up and grab the doorknob to go back inside.

But I stop myself.

I am the lookout. This is my job.

I *am* good for something.

As I stand here, I scan the art that's taped on the walls next to our door. Ms. Bryce always put the best art from class on the wall, but none of it is mine. There are bird pictures from Eric, Paige, Madelyn, Giovanna, Adam, Lizzie, and others.

I don't think I ever finished my picture. I was too busy goofing off.

A couple of kids drew pictures of woodpeckers. Woodpeckers are pretty interesting unless you have a wooden leg or wooden teeth or you're a wooden puppet like Pinocchio. Then, woodpeckers can be scary.

I walk down the hallway, looking at artwork from other classes. Mr. Paul's class drew self-portraits. Some are really good, and some are not. One kid has three ears, and I wonder if that was on purpose or by accident.

Mrs. Emery's class has poems outside her door. The poems are all about family, like, "I love my mother. And also my brother."

I could write a better poem about my family.

At home it's a ruckus, the place such a mess—
Why, things are calmer at school during recess.
With the five of us kids there's always commotion,
But I'll change—just watch! And Mom will get her
*   promotion.*

I'm still on the other end of the hallway when I see Mrs. Duncan. She's our librarian. Her heels clop on the floor, echoing.

She stops walking right in front of our classroom.

I'm supposed to be the lookout. I've messed up again.

I really am good for nothing.

"Hi, Mrs. Duncan," I call, waving and rushing over. "I was just, um, in the bathroom."

She looks at me, wagging her finger. "There's no running in the hallways, Kyle," she says. I slow down. "Is everything all right?" she asks. "I haven't seen Ms. Bryce since Monday."

"Everything is great!" I say, smiling.

"Your class is being very loud."

"Sorry about that. We're working on a science experiment with vinegar and temperature and things," I babble, hoping it'll drive her away. "It really smells in there."

Thankfully, my excuse works, and Mrs. Duncan nods and turns from the door. With a clop, clop, she disappears around the corner.

As my heart pounds in my chest at a trillion beats a second, I slink down to the floor, right below the woodpecker pictures.

I'm starting to think that it's a lot harder *not* having a teacher than having one.

15
SAMANTHA

Giovanna wears a new cream T-shirt, but it's so not her color. With her milky-white skin, she should be wearing deep reds, icy pastels, and dark blues. I hand her a magazine. "Page eighty-two," I say, pointing to the headline highlighted on the cover. "The article on skin tone and colors." Giovanna nods gratefully.

That girl is lucky I'm here to help her.

As she opens the magazine, Giovanna knocks a card off her desk. She quickly bends over, picks it up, and stuffs it inside her notebook. I saw Jade and Jasmine with the same cards, too. They are from Emmy. I think she's having a birthday party. I might be the only girl in class who is not invited.

Not that I want to go to her party, anyway. I have nothing in common with most of those girls.

Still. You'd think she'd invite me. I'm always going out of my way to help everyone. Just the other week I suggested Emmy should wear skinnier jeans.

She frowned and turned away without even thanking me. But I was just trying to help. Like this morning, when I complained to Aunt Karen that she needed to make her freshly squeezed orange juice more carefully. There was too much pulp swimming inside the glass, so I couldn't drink it. Aunt Karen told me I was too picky.

Maybe some advice is best left unshared.

I'll need to think about that.

Like, my fashion magazines always make fun of out-of-style celebrity fashion. But maybe what's funny in magazines is sort of mean face-to-face.

I look away from Giovanna. Kyle is back from his outside-the-room lookout post and Trevor has taken his place. Kyle opens Soda's cage, lifts up the rodent, and tosses it at Jasmine.

Ugh! I can't imagine anything worse than a rodent in my hair.

Kyle laughs. He still has Soda—he was only pretending to throw it. That's a good thing for Jasmine.

And I suppose it's a good thing for the rodent, too.

I turn my attention back to Giovanna. She stands up to adjust her shirt, which is tucked into her jeans. It really should be untucked. I open my mouth to tell her, but then bite my lip and instead say, "I really like your shirt. Is it new?"

Giovanna smiles brightly. "It is. Thanks!"

Her smile makes me smile, too. Then I notice the invitation

to Emmy's party sticking out of her notebook, just slightly. I avert my eyes, but my smile vanishes.

My notebook is stuffed with new assignments from Maggie. There are way too many. Last night I needed Aunt Karen's help in finishing them. Mom and Dad were too busy, as usual. I finished so late I didn't have a chance to check out my favorite fashion blogs online, and I *always* have time for that.

"I keep thinking we're missing something big," says Giovanna to me.

"Like nail polish? We can talk that if you want," I say, hopeful.

Giovanna frowns. "No, I mean we're missing something big in class. There's something happening soon. But I can't remember what."

"I wouldn't worry," I say. "Maggie's got everything under control."

An eraser lands on my desk, only inches from my arm. Seth grabs it. "Sorry," he blurts out. He smirks and then whips the eraser at Kyle, who bumps into Danny's desk as he tries to duck. Danny looks up, annoyed.

I *think* Maggie has everything under control, anyway.

"Well, let me know if you want to talk about nails. Or jewelry," I say to Giovanna, looking at her small golden stud earrings that cry out, *Starter earrings.* "I have some suggestions," I say, but then catch myself and force a smile. "Not that you need any," I quickly add.

16
MAGGIE

Being a teacher is exhausting and tiring, an effort of near Herculean proportions. Hercules was this mythological strong man who performed twelve heroic labors, but I bet none were as tough as grading homework. I stayed up past midnight last night, and I'll probably have to work all weekend. I thought being a teacher would be a breeze and a half. I was wrong, and that's not something that happens often, if ever.

My classmates make so many mistakes and their handwriting is messy. In math, we are supposed to show our work, but it's nearly impossible to figure out what half the class is doing and how they get their answers.

Emmy got question number five right on math work sheet seven, but purely by accident, using multiplication and subtraction, when you were supposed to divide. Do I give her credit for the question or not? And what about Eli, who used the right formula but then wrote a three instead of a five for the final answer because his handwriting is so messy he probably couldn't read it correctly? Does he get partial credit? Full credit?

But grading the work is only part of my responsibilities. I need to create lesson plans and homework every day, too. We can't go a day without learning.

I, Maggie Cranberry, will not waste a day of learning.

I admit it—Ms. Bryce's job was not as easy as I thought. No wonder she was always in a bad mood. Harvard University better appreciate the work I'm doing, that's all I can say.

But I'll muddle through, somehow. I simply have to. Everyone's depending on me, whether they know it or not. Mom and Dad will be so proud. I'll probably skip high school and go right to Harvard, where they'll name a building after me. I can see it now—cheerleaders jumping outside as I walk to the brand-new Maggie Cranberry Hall, news cameras flashing and a thousand people cheering my name: *Maggie! Maggie! Maggie!* Kyle is there, and he's cheering, too. I couldn't miss his bright red hair even if I wanted to. He walks up to me, and he looks into my eyes, and I look back at his—

I jerk my eyes open. Did I fall asleep for a moment? No wonder adults drink coffee to stay awake in the morning after working late at night, even though the stuff smells like motor oil.

Kyle is standing at my desk. I shake the lingering images of my dream from my mind. "Yes?" I ask after clearing my throat.

Kyle holds one of my assignment sheets. It's the one on invertebrates I handed out. Those are animals without spines, like insects, worms, clams, and snails.

"You gave me a C," he says, pointing at the page. He jabs at it. He looks angry.

"I have to grade the papers," I explain. "If I don't, our parents will think something is wrong."

"But I got all the questions right."

I slide on my glasses, which I had removed to rub my eyes right before I fell asleep, if I fell asleep. I'm not entirely admitting that I fell asleep, only that the possibility exists. Kyle glares at me with his bright green orbs. I look away from him, embarrassed by my dream, and scan his sheet. "Right. You did. But your parents might be curious about why you are suddenly getting good grades," I explain. "We have to maintain appearances."

"I spent a lot of time on this homework," Kyle protests.

"This isn't about you. One false move and Harvard won't name a building after me!" Kyle squints and narrows his eyes. Did I just say that? I'm more tired than I thought. I clear my throat. "I mean, our teacher-free holiday will be over. *That's* what's important, of course. We all have to make sacrifices."

Kyle snatches his paper from my grasp and clomps back to his seat. When he gets there, he throws an eraser at one of his goony friends.

I think of my dream and shudder. If I'm dreaming of Kyle Anderson, I'm really losing my mind.

I yawn and push open the skin around my eyes, trying to wake myself up. Then I scan the pile of paper I removed from Ms. Bryce's files this morning. According to her plans, we're supposed to learn about the American Revolution; fractions, division, and geometry; photosynthesis and living organisms; and a lot more. Some of these things I haven't learned yet. How am I supposed to teach things I haven't learned?

I'll need to stay up all weekend and study. Class 507 is depending on me.

Besides, winter break will be here soon. I'll sleep then, after my family visits Harvard.

I'm looking through the paper stack when I notice a blue piece of paper, stuck to another blue page so I didn't see it before. The wording at the top looks vaguely familiar. It reads: A Reminder about Fifth Grade Presents Night.

Fifth Grade Presents Night. My muddled, sleep-deprived brain tosses those words back and forth. Where have I heard them before?

Oh no! I remember *now*. I brought home a flyer from school the other week for my parents. I didn't think much about it. That was the same day we got my big book on the history of Harvard.

A wad of worry-filled saliva fills my throat, and a horrible twisting feeling settles in my stomach. How could I forget about *this*?

This is enormous, mountainous, mega-gigantic elephantine times infinity huge.

In other words, *this* is big.

The more I read, the tighter my stomach twists.

Fifth Grade Presents . . . The American Revolution!

The after-school activity night is next Friday.

The paper—a personal note from Principal Klein—reminds each and every teacher his or her class is responsible for a specific activity during the event.

Mrs. Greeley's class is in charge of selling concessions (American-themed!).

Mr. Foley's class will sing an authentic American Revolution song, with drums.

Mrs. Crawford's class will take care of the decorations and clean up afterward.

Ms. Bryce's class will perform an original play.

When I read that last line, my lips tremble. We're to perform a class play in front of everyone? An *original* play? Our class has the hardest job!!

My hands shake so much I can barely thumb through her papers. Ms. Bryce must have a script she wrote somewhere.

Our teacher—sorry, our former teacher—files everything carefully. So where is it?

I look under *A* for *American* and *R* for *Revolution* in her alphabetized files. I look in the front and the back. I look behind the files, in case it fell. I would look on her computer, but most of her files are password protected, and I've already tried every password I could imagine.

I can't find anything, anywhere. Not one mention of a play. Not a scene, not an act, not a single word. Nothing.

We're doomed.

There goes Harvard. No way they'll accept me with this failure on my record. Mom and Dad are going to be crushed. I'll be the first Cranberry in one hundred years not to be admitted.

I'll be lucky to make it to middle school.

In the back of the room, Brian throws an eraser at Seth. Maybe I should join them. If my future is doomed, I might as well start a life as a juvenile delinquent.

"We're ready to pick pencils for detention," says Paige, approaching my desk. I groan and look up. Other kids are gathered around, too. "What's wrong? You look kind of sick. Do you want me to help you?"

Her eyebrows rise, eager to help, but I shake my head. "I'm fine."

"Are you sure? I can create a work sheet or two, you know."

"No, no, no," I insist, my voice raspy and cracking. My

mouth is so dry I can barely speak. I grab the pencils from my desk and hold out my hands for the class.

My classmates gather around me to choose. One hand reaches in after another. In a moment, all the pencils are gone and everyone looks to see who will go to the principal's office.

It's Adam. He has grabbed the short pencil again. He moans.

But we're all in much, much bigger trouble than that.

17
ADAM

I pulled the short pencil for detention. Again. When Ms. Bryce left, I thought I was done with detention. I figured that, finally, I wouldn't get in any more trouble for no good reason at all.

But I'm sent to the principal's office just as often as I was before. No, I'm sent to his office *more* often than before.

I've always been the best-behaved kid in class, too. I'm just blamed for stuff. Like the time I left the faucet going in the lab sink and it overflowed and ruined the floor and Ms. Bryce's shoes.

It's not like I left the paper towel in the sink on purpose. How I was supposed to know it would clog the drain like that? I was trying to clean the sink and do a good deed. I just forgot the towel was there.

"Anyone want to switch with me?" I ask. "I went to the office yesterday. And the day before that." And the day before that.

I hold up my short pencil and scan the room. No one steps forward or raises their hand. Not that I can blame them. It isn't any fun getting into trouble.

Maggie doesn't look at me. She just pulls her hair and stares at the walls. I don't know why she's so upset. It's not like she's the one marching to the principal's office again.

My eyes meet Lizzie's. I think that she is about to open her mouth and raise her hand. I shake my head.

No. I am not switching with Lizzie. I wouldn't want *her* to get into trouble, even if it's fake trouble.

Lizzie shrugs and smiles at me. I'd happily get into all sorts of trouble for that smile.

I'll grab another lollipop for her while I'm in the office. She told me she likes grape the best. I'll grab two grape lollipops. Maybe three. It's my favorite flavor, too. At least it's my favorite flavor now.

Ms. Bryce kept a detention slip pad on her desk. Before I head out the door, I tear a slip from the pad. But I need to think of a reason why I'm in trouble. I can't just report to the principal's office for no reason at all.

The first time, I forgot to bring a slip. So when I got to the office and Mrs. Frank asked me for it, I froze.

"Hand it over," she said.

I didn't respond.

"I need your slip." She held out her hand.

I stammered. "Uh, I don't have one."

She tapped her pencil on her notepad. "Why not?" she asked.

I bit my tongue. "It's because . . ." I fidgeted. "It's because I ate the detention pad," I blurted out. "And that's why I'm in trouble."

Mrs. Frank frowned. "And why did you eat the detention pad?"

"Um . . . Because I wanted to take a bite out of crime?"

She sighed and told me to take a seat.

So this time, I make sure I'm prepared. It's not easy to make up things that will get you in trouble, but not in *too* much trouble. I can't claim to do anything that will trigger a phone call to my parents.

I jot down an excuse and head toward the door.

"I'm reporting to the principal's office," I say, stopping at the door frame. "It's not too late to switch with me." But no one even looks at me except Lizzie, who smiles. I sigh and leave.

I'm just glad today is Friday so I can't possibly be sent to detention tomorrow. At least I think I can't.

If anyone asks me, I'm not pulling any pencils on Saturday.

When I arrive at the office, Mrs. Frank looks up from her computer screen. "What is it now, Adam?" she asks, tapping her pencil on her notepad.

I hand her my slip.

She reads it, shakes her head, and then looks up at me. "It says you ate Lizzie's homework."

I nod.

"Why would you do that?"

"I heard the assignment was a piece of cake."

She moans. "You have a nasty habit of eating things." She points to the row of green plastic chairs against the wall and across from her desk. "Principal Klein will be with you in a few minutes. Have a seat. And try not to eat anything."

18

ERIC

Maggie sits at the teacher's desk, pulling at her hair. I try to hand her my homework. I'm not sure why I did all the homework when a teacher isn't assigning it.

That's not true; I know exactly why I did it. I did the homework because everyone else was doing the homework, and I didn't want to stick out.

As I hold my pages in front of her, Maggie barely blinks an eye. She waves to a stack of papers on the desk and I rest my sheets on it. Maggie glances at the pile and sighs.

I sit down, ready to write another story. I'm in the same seat Ms. Bryce assigned to me on the first day of class: fourth row, second from the right. Most other kids have changed their seats. There's no one to tell us we *can't* switch seats.

Most desks are not even in rows anymore. Some face each other in pairs, and other desks are in clusters of various sizes, like the six girls to my left who have formed a small circle.

The Big Goofs own the far corner, their desks spread out so they can hurl erasers at one another.

I haven't moved my desk an inch. I have nowhere to move it to.

I write a story about a classroom with desks that move. I call it "The Enchanted Classroom." Every morning the kids in Class 507 find their desks in different places and have to slide the desks back into their correct spots.

A boy decides to find out what's happening. So one night, instead of going home, he hides in the classroom closet. He doesn't tell anyone. Eventually, he falls asleep, but scraping sounds across the floor wake him up late in the night.

Every night, the desks come to life. They talk and move around.

One desk says, "I'm tired of Jimmy Jones sticking gum under my desk. I should stick gum on him!"

Another desk whines, "That's nothing. Felicia White draws on me every day. How do you think she'd feel if I drew on *her*?"

The hiding boy sneezes, and the desks discover him in the closet. They snap their tops up and down. The boy cowers as the desks move closer. THOMP! THOMP! Their tops bang faster and faster. THOMP! THOMP! THOMP!

"He knows we're alive. We can't let him escape," says the teacher's desk, which is their leader.

The next day, the boy is missing, but oddly, the teacher's desk looks bigger than it did the day before, and in the middle of class it burps.

I stop writing when I notice Maggie standing up. She's in front of the class, banging a stapler on a desk. She looks tired and worn down, with bags under her eyes.

"Maggie—are you okay?" Lacey asks.

"We're doomed," sobs Maggie.

Maggie clears her throat. She has everyone's attention. Even Brian stops to look at her, his arm about to chuck an eraser, but frozen midchuck.

Maggie holds up a piece of paper and waves it in the air. "Do you know what this is?" she asks.

"A piece of paper?" suggests Seth. He and Brian laugh.

Maggie ignores them. "It's a note," she wails, her voice quivering. "A note written by our own Principal Klein. It's dated two weeks ago."

"So?" asks Gavin.

"According to the note, we have to perform a class play next Friday night. One week from today," she gulps. "One week. That's ten thousand minutes or so. Well, a little bit more than that, since we're performing Friday *evening*. So about ten thousand five hundred minutes if my math is correct, and I'm sure it is. Ten thousand five hundred minutes until our doom!" she cries. She rubs her eyes as tears roll down her face. "I don't know what we're going to do."

"We'll perform a play," says Seth. "That doesn't sound hard. What play?"

"We don't have a play!" complains Maggie. "That's part of the problem. Maybe Ms. Bryce was going to write it, I think. I don't know. But we have to perform this *original* play in front of all our parents in one week. We can't perform a play that doesn't exist.

"When Principal Klein finds out, he'll probably make all of us repeat fifth grade," she continues. She lowers the page and the tears roll down her cheeks like a rainstorm. She blows her nose on her sleeve. "All my plans! Ruined!"

Brian drops his eraser. His mouth is open and his eyes are wide. "Did you say we might have to repeat fifth grade?" he barks, a violent tone to his voice.

"My father wouldn't stand for it," says Samantha, folding her arms across her chest.

"I want to go to middle school next year," complains Madelyn.

"I didn't do anything wrong!" laments Paige.

As other kids cry out with complaints and concerns, Maggie crumples to the ground as if she's a house of cards that blew over.

"Let's just skip it," says Seth. "We'll tell the principal we fell asleep or something."

"We'll tell Principal Klein the entire class fell asleep for an entire month?" Lacey asks.

"He'll never believe *that*," says Paige.

"Let's hire a professional theater group to write and perform a play in our place," Samantha suggests. "My dad will pay for it."

"I think Principal Klein will notice if a professional theater troupe performs instead of us," says Maggie.

"Fine. Whatever." Samantha turns her head and sniffs, as if she's just been insulted. "I'm just trying to help."

Some kids moan, others sigh. Everyone looks at one another.

"Um, so, what if we write the play ourselves?" I ask. "We still have time, right?"

Maggie's tears turn off. She looks up from the floor. "Maybe. I don't know. Who would write it?"

People look at me, and I immediately wish that I had kept my mouth shut. I slink low in my chair, trying to disappear from the stares. I wish my mouth were supergluegummed shut.

No one can write an entire play over a weekend, can they?

But then again, maybe someone could. I bet I could. Writing a play would be sort of fun, actually. Sure, it would be a lot of work, but I'd probably do a great job. I inch my hand up slowly. I feel like a flower that's about to be picked, and it's not a good feeling. As my hand lifts, my stomach knots.

"I'll write it," Kyle calls out.

Kyle? He's just about the last person I'd expect to volunteer for this.

Still, I quickly lower my inched-up hand.

"You?" asks Maggie, her mouth gaping.

Kyle nods. "Of course. Why not me?"

I can think of a million reasons why not Kyle. But I keep them to myself.

I'm just relieved no one saw me about to raise my arm.

19

SAMANTHA

Walking home, I pass the Building Where the Old Blue Hairs Live (my new name for the old folks' home next door). I don't even realize I'm walking by it, because my head is down and I'm so busy wondering what's going to happen in school with our class play and if it will expose our secret.

Not that it would make a difference to me. Daddy has way too much money for something like this to have any sort of lasting impact on my future. But Maggie seemed pretty devastated. I bet Giovanna would be upset, too. A lot of kids would be very disappointed if our secret spilled.

All of the girls in class would probably complain about it at Emmy's upcoming birthday party, the one that I'm not invited to attend. Or maybe the party would be canceled if our secret got out. Not that I care about a stupid birthday party, either.

Well, maybe I care a little.

That's strange. I mean, I don't care about most of the other girls in class, not really. At least, not very much.

But maybe I care because sharing a really huge secret is sort of like being in a big, private, cozy club together, like Daddy's country club, but with secrets.

Or maybe it's something else, and maybe that something else doesn't have anything to do with money or country clubs or even our boat.

I'm too busy thinking about all of *that*, so I'm not paying attention to the Big House with Ancient People Stuffed Inside (ha! I like that name better) when Mr. Wolcott's loud voice shouts out to me. "Franny! Shall I compare thee to a summer's day?" He waves to me, stretching out his arm as if he's performing in front of a packed house and not sitting on a lawn chair.

"I'm not Franny. I'm Samantha," I remind him, rolling my eyes.

"Yes, of course. But you could be twins. Oh, I loved her! She lit up the stage as if she were the only one under the spotlight, and the other players merely props." He gestures with one hand, sweeping it across the air. "Oh, my bounty for her is as boundless as the sea. But as they say, men at some time are masters of their fates."

No one says that, but I just nod and mumble, "Sure, whatever."

I give him a wave to go, but I turn to look at him. Don't get me wrong. Mr. Wolcott is sweet and all, but I always sort of brush by him with a half glance. Most days, I'm in a hurry to get home.

I fight the urge to criticize his necktie, which is way too wide to be in fashion, but keep my stare locked into his eyes. Normally, they twinkle, but today they look dull. His bright blue eyes seem misted by a haze.

"Anything wrong, Mr. Wolcott?" I ask.

He smiles, and his eyes dance back to life. "No. Nothing. It's her birthday today, that is all."

"Whose birthday? Franny Bree's?" I guess, and Mr. Wolcott nods. "How come you guys never married?"

He shakes his head. He looks away, as if he can see her right in front of him. Maybe he can, sort of. "We were young. She met another. Perhaps it was not meant to be."

I want to tell him that he'll meet someone else, but I'm guessing at his age those days are gone. "I'm sorry," I say, and I am. I wish Daddy could buy him a little less loneliness, but I have a feeling that wouldn't really work.

But I can't stay and chat. I have a very busy afternoon ahead. I need to hurry upstairs, eat a snack, and change clothes for ballet class. Then, I have violin lessons. And tonight I really, really, really need to go online and look for new shoes to match my red backpack.

"I'll see you around, Mr. Wolcott," I say. "I've got to run. Cheer up!"

Mr. Wolcott smiles at me, his eyes once again twinkling. "Parting is such sweet sorrow!" he calls out.

When I get up to our apartment, Aunt Karen has lemonade waiting for me on the table. There aren't many things better than lemonade, especially when there's a wedge of lemon on the edge of the glass and one of those little fancy umbrellas poked into it. I put my lips on the end of the bendy straw and take a sip.

I put the glass down and push it away from me.

"What's wrong?" asks my aunt.

It's way too watery. It needs more sugar, too. "Drinking this is such sour sorrow," I mutter.

"What was that, Samantha?"

"Nothing," I say. I take another sip of the lemonade and fake a happy grin. "Mmmm. Delicious!"

20
KYLE

As I walk down my apartment building hallway, I still cannot believe I'm going to write the class play.

Me, Kyle Anderson: serious screwup turned sensational scribe.

Yow. Yow. Yow.

I'll double that. Yow. Yow. Yow. Yow. Yow. Yow.

I've never written a play before. But I bet I can do it, even though it'll be hard work.

Yow. Yow.

I'm up for the challenge.

Yow?

Everyone in class was mega-surprised I volunteered. I could see it in their faces, their pursed lips and popping eyeballs.

Maggie's expression was the most priceless. She looked like she had swallowed a frog.

I expected her to croak on the spot.

Everyone thinks that all I do is horse around with Brian and Seth. And maybe they are right.

Were right.

No more.

I'll show them that I'm more than a horrible horse-around goof-off. I'll show my mom, too.

Besides, writing a play can't be much harder than writing rhymes, right?

The play was amazing, everyone said.

That boy's got some brains hidden in his red head.

There's a voice inside my head telling me that I can do this, too. It says that I *can* be an ace student. I can be serious *and* reliable.

And for once, I'm not telling the voice to *shut up.*

I'm going to write the greatest play ever. I'll be a whole new Kyle, a Kyle who's good for *something.*

I barely notice the smell of curry in the hallway as I turn the doorknob to enter our apartment. It's quiet in the hall, but when the door swings open, I'm immediately hit by the sounds of my siblings wailing and the TV blaring and an unpleasant stink that reminds me of dirty diapers.

In the kitchen, Mom feeds AJ, although she probably has more food on the floor than in his mouth. The green dots on Mom's face must be smashed peas. At least I hope that's what they are.

Leah sits on the floor, banging a wooden spoon against the base of the table.

"Can you keep an eye on AJ?" Mom asks, wiping peas off his face. She lifts him from the high chair and puts him on the floor.

"Sure," I say.

But I need to get started on writing my play, too.

I have responsibilities.

No more goofing off for me.

I grab a handful of lined paper and a pencil from our junk drawer, scoop up AJ in my other arm, and head to the family room. Marley and Nate watch cartoons. I put AJ on the carpet, and he immediately starts whacking the sofa with a rattle that was lying next to him.

"Keep it down," says Marley, but AJ keeps banging. I nudge him with my leg so that he's hitting the fabric of the sofa and not its leg. This way the whacking is not nearly as distracting.

But at least the banging will keep him busy for a while.

I sit on the big recliner. There's a small writing table next to it. I lay my paper on the table and hold up my pencil, ready to begin writing.

I jot my name on the top of the page, big, like John Hancock big. (John Hancock is famous for signing his name in a gigantic size on the Declaration of Independence. I'll have to put that in my play. I wonder what rhymes with *gigantic*?)

I peek at the television only a few times. Mostly, I stare at the paper—the white piece of paper staring back at me. It's practically daring me to write on it.

My name remains big. The rest of the page remains empty.

I think about everything I know of the American Revolution. George Washington cut down a cherry tree and had wooden teeth. I wonder if he was scared of woodpeckers? Also, there was a tea party. Paul Revere rode a horse to warn people. I think they picked him because no one else owned a horse. Betsy Ross sewed the flag. I wonder how she knew to add fifty stars, one for each state? That must have been a lucky guess because I don't think they had fifty states yet. I'm pretty sure Alaska and Hawaii came later. Ben Franklin was also involved somehow. He discovered electricity, too. I wonder if he had magic electrical superpowers.

I put down my pencil in frustration. What was I thinking? What do I know about writing a play? What do I really know about the American Revolution?

America revolted. Doing work is revolting.

And I'm stuck.

It'll take all weekend to write this!

But I made a promise.

I will no longer be an undependable oaf. I'm a new Kyle. If I can't do *this*, how can I expect to take care of my brothers and sisters while Mom is working a new job?

I will write the play! Me! Make no mistake—
And I'll start it after this commercial break.

On the TV, Squiggle Cat gets poked in the eye. I laugh. "Yow, yow, yow!" he hollers.

Sometime later, I'm not sure how much later, Mom sticks her head in the room. She's still covered in peas and I have to keep from laughing. One is mashed onto the tip of her nose, like a wart. She looks like the Wicked Witch of the West.

"Where's AJ?" she asks.

"He's right next to me."

"Where?" Mom asks.

I look down at the floor. AJ *was* right next to me.

Uh-oh.

I bolt out of the chair. AJ was here a minute ago. Or maybe it was many minutes ago. He couldn't have gone far, right? My brother can't even walk yet. He has to be in the apartment somewhere. Somewhere safe.

"How long has the front door been open like that?" Mom asks.

The front door to our apartment is wide open. Did I close it when I came home today? I can't remember.

My mind fills with panic. I run out into the hallway, but I don't see AJ at all. He's vanished.

At the far end of the hallway a small door is open. It's the garbage chute door.

Oh no.

I sprint down the hall. "AJ?" I yell out. "Are you there?" When I get to the chute, I poke my head as far as I can inside the metal tube. "AJ? Can you hear me?"

My voice echoes through the metallic passageway. It travels down, down, down to the basement.

No voice bounces back.

The garbage chute opens up into a large, rusty metal container filled with everyone's trash. AJ could be in the container right now. He could have slid down the shaft and landed in the container.

He could have hit his head. He could be trying to eat a plastic bag.

I don't want to think what I'm thinking.

I was going to be a new Kyle! A better Kyle! Instead, I'm as good for nothing as I always have been.

I don't wait for Mom. I fling open the stairway door and dash down the stairs, two at a time, down the three flights all the way to the basement.

I've only been in the garbage room once before, when I accidentally threw away Mom's watch last year. It took some time, but I found that watch and it was only a little dented.

The thought makes me feel worse. What if AJ is a little dented?

As I step off the final stair, the hum of a radiator fills the air. It's dark, cold, and damp. I'm too worried to be scared, although it's extremely scary down here, with moisture on the gray concrete slabs and some sort of creaking coming from the vents. I wouldn't be surprised if rats live down here. It feels like the sort of place rats live. The lights are dim and cobwebs are everywhere. The stale trash stench is overpowering.

"AJ?" I cry out.

Please answer me, please answer me!

I wait for a response.

I don't get one, except for the slight echo of my voice.

The container is open but taller than me. I need to stand on my tiptoes and hoist myself up on the side of the container to peek in.

I'm scared at what I might find.

But I find nothing.

The container is empty except for the old garbage smell and multicolored dark stains caked into the metal sides: reds, greens, and browns. "AJ?"

Maybe the trash has already been emptied and thrown into a truck. Maybe I just missed it. Right now AJ could be sitting in the rear of a garbage truck, being hauled off to a dump somewhere.

We need to call the trash company. The police. The fire department! I sprint back up the stairs. It's a lot harder running up stairs than it is running down them, but I don't have time to take it easy.

By the time I reach our floor, I'm breathing heavily. I plow across the hallway to our apartment. I can't catch my breath.

I inhale giant whiffs of curry as I pass apartment 3F. I wheeze.

When I push open our apartment door, Mom is in the kitchen with AJ, rocking him in her arms. He looks fine. He coos.

"He was in the bathroom," Mom says. "Eating soap."

I have never been more thankful for anything in my life.

Mom glares at me, her eyes angry, but I think she's too relieved to yell at me just now. I'm sure I'll be yelled at later.

I mutter an apology and, with my shoulders slumping, lumber to the family room. I stand in the doorway. Marley and Nate are still watching cartoons.

Squiggle Cat gets poked in the eye, but I don't laugh.

I was supposed to do something else right now, something for school, but I can barely think straight. I'm just glad AJ is fine. Anything else can wait until after I watch this show, or maybe it can wait until the show after that.

I hear my mom's voice behind me. She's talking to AJ, not me, using her calm, soothing voice. But her words stick in my stomach and bury themselves in there. "And that's why I can't leave you guys alone and take that promotion, honey," she says, to herself more than him.

I don't think Mom intended for me to hear that, but I feel like I'm going to be sick.

21
MAGGIE

On Monday, Kyle strolls into class with a big, blockhead grin. He looks exactly the opposite of how I feel. Last night I dreamed I was Chicken Little. But in my dream the sky *was* falling and no one listened to me. Which is most definitely not how the story goes.

Over the weekend, Mom and I talked about our Harvard trip. She told me we could still change our plans and head somewhere more fun. I told her I still wanted to go, but I know, in my heart, that it doesn't really matter. Harvard won't admit me when they discover I'm a liar and a failure at directing plays and at leading blockheads.

I'm a blockhead, too. I'm probably the biggest blockhead of all. My future was so bright, but now it's shrouded in so much pitch-black darkness, I need a flashlight to see it.

"Do you need any help?" Paige asks me. Lacey stands behind her.

"I'm quite fine, thank you," I say, but I say it louder and with a more irritated tone than I intend. They turn and walk away and I wonder, for a fleeting moment, if I should call them back. I feel bad, but then Kyle strolls up with a thick pile of stapled papers. My chance to smooth things over with my friends vanishes.

"It's done," says Kyle.

"What's done?" I stare at him blankly.

"The play," he says. "I wrote it. Stapled, collated, and ready to roll."

I raise my eyebrows. The play is typed. It's complete. And—fit for hundreds of parents to watch? I'm stunned, but dubious.

Dubious means I'm doubtful, uncertain, and cannot believe a Neanderthal like Kyle came through for us.

My spirits lift a little. Just a little, though.

This *is* goofball Kyle we're talking about.

"It's a musical," he says. "Everyone loves a musical, right?"

I nod slowly. Musicals are whimsical, bouncy nothings. The American Revolution was not whimsical, bouncy, and certainly not nothing. My slightly elevated spirits start to plunge back to their sub-basement level.

I stare at the title page: *Let Liberty Fall: A Musical about Teeth and Freedom.*

"A musical about teeth?" I ask, puzzled.

"Sure. You know, I call it *Let Liberty Fall* because of our town name, Liberty Falls. That's pretty clever, right? But then there's George Washington. He had wooden teeth, right? That was a huge part of the American Revolution. Along with Ben Franklin's superpowers and all the tea parties everyone had."

"Um, I don't think so," I mutter. My spirits plunge back into a pit of total black doom. "Did you spend a lot of time writing this?"

"Of course. I mean, I guess it sort of depends on what you mean by 'a lot.'" He laughs, but I don't join in his merriment.

I keep one copy of the script and hand the rest of the pile back to Kyle to share with the class. I read the first page, and any remaining hope I had shrivel up into a bitter and stomach-churning seed of despair. I shake my head.

Wrong. Wrong. Wrong.

I continue reading, and the seed lurking in my stomach grows and grows until it's the size of a large, overripe pumpkin. This play is filled with fabrications, mistakes, and utter nonsense. George Washington did *not* build the George Washington Bridge, and if he did, he certainly didn't cross it to fight the British. Abraham Lincoln did not invent the top hat, and he wasn't even alive during the Revolutionary War. Half the play is about Washington's wooden teeth.

The play isn't totally worthless, though. There's a scene between George and Martha Washington that's sort of touching, as Martha tries to persuade George to lead the army. There's a rousing song by the Freedom Fighters as they vow to fight for their independence. His lyrics aren't half bad.

Some of the wooden teeth stuff is funny, kind of, if you like that sort of thing.

Not that the Revolutionary War was funny. Freedom is not a laughing matter.

I had imagined a dramatic retelling of our Founding Fathers' struggles against the overbearing British government. Taxation without representation! The demanding king, oblivious to our plight, flexes his muscles until we are forced to rebel!

Instead, I get a silly play about wooden teeth.

And then there's the ending, where Benjamin Franklin flies a kite during a thunderstorm, lightning strikes and gives him superpowers, and he uses them to help defeat the British army.

I'm pretty sure that didn't happen.

I glare at Kyle. His big grin starts to fade. "What?"

"Did you do *any* research?" I ask.

His piercing green eyes flicker. He wrinkles his nose, which gives him the cutest little *who me?* sort of look. I force myself to maintain my stern glare, anyway.

As the classroom teacher, I need to be firm.

Kyle looks down at the floor. "Well, I wanted to do more research. But I lost track of time, a little bit. I can make some changes."

"Do that. And lose the second part of the title, okay? The teeth part."

My stomach, which was already in knots, becomes knottier. I feel bad as Kyle stomps away. Was I too harsh? But we're performing Friday. *This* Friday. If we perform the play as written, we're doomed.

Kyle will have to make it better, that's all. I wish I had more faith in him. If only he weren't such a blockhead, even if he's a cute blockhead. I don't have time to rewrite this myself, either. I could save it, probably. Maybe. But I have papers to grade, tests to give, and homework to assign. And the script is only a small part of a play. There are props! Costumes! Direction!

If someone else could help, things would be easier. But as the teacher of this class, I must supervise *everything*. I must lead. I must take control. Everyone's depending on me, me, me, and *me*!

I mean, right?

I clear my throat, trying to remove the great lump that lingers inside it. I stand up and slam my stapler against the desk to get the class's attention. I speak in my most measured yet authoritative tone. "Thank you for the play, Kyle. Your take on the American Revolution is . . . um, very interesting."

Kyle sits with a half frown.

"We must move forward," I continue. "We'll have to cast the parts. Who will play George Washington, our first president, and hero of the American Revolution?"

Brian raises his hand, and for a moment I'm torn between happiness that we have a volunteer and total panic that the volunteer is Brian. He would be awful in the role. But then I see that Brian is holding an eraser, which he tosses at Seth's head. He wasn't volunteering at all.

No one else moves.

"Someone has to be George Washington," I plead. Still, no one raises a hand. "Fine. We'll draw pencils."

I order everyone to gather around me as I remove our pencils from my desk. I extend my fist holding the pencils, the broken one mixed among them.

My classmates slide them out, one by one.

"Not me!" says Brian.

"Not me!" says Trevor.

"I've got it," says Adam, showing everyone the short pencil in his fingers. "I'll be George Washington, I guess."

His moan is met with smiles and breaths of relief from the other kids.

That's one part down, but we have many to go. "Who wants to be Martha Washington?" I ask.

Lizzie raises her hand. "Me!"

Good. That was easy.

Lizzie looks at Adam, and he looks back at her. They smile at each other. They hold their gaze way too long.

Gross.

"I have some script ideas," says Lizzie, gazing at Adam. "We need to add some romance to the play."

"Good idea," says Adam.

I roll my eyes as I distribute the other parts. Now the volunteers come easily. Cooper will play Thomas Jefferson. Emmy nabs the role of Betsy Ross. Other kids play John Hancock, Ben Franklin, Paul Revere, and various towns-people. I look around at the rest of the class and assign them roles, too. Samantha and Giovanna will create the sets. Kyle will work on revising the script. Seth and Brian will, apparently, continue to hurl erasers at each other.

I give them parts as British redcoats. They can hurl erasers at the colonists or something.

Two quick warning knocks come from outside the door. I jump. Fortunately, Jade is in the hallway, at her lookout post, right where she should be. We scurry to our seats, and I rush to my old desk. The chair is cold. It feels small. I'm unused to such cramped seating.

But I can't be seen at the teacher's desk, even if it's where I belong.

Principal Klein strolls into the room. He scans us, one by

one, but we sit up straight and smile. There is no goofing off here. Not on my watch! His eyes settle on Ms. Bryce's empty chair. "Where's your teacher?"

I gulp, and I wonder if Principal Klein can hear my gulp, it's so loud. My head starts to fill with new worry. But then Eric says, "She's in the bathroom."

"Why is she always in the bathroom?" asks Principal Klein. He looks genuinely concerned.

We all shrug.

Principal Klein sighs. "Just let her know we need the permission slips for your field trip tomorrow."

"Field trip?" I squawk.

22

ERIC

Principal Klein stands in front of our classroom doorway. He has just announced we have a field trip tomorrow. With all the excitement over the last few days, I completely forgot about our trip.

I think we all completely forgot about it.

"Of course!" our principal says. "A field trip to the Liberty Falls History Museum. Aren't you excited?"

I wouldn't use the word *excited* to describe our mood right now. I think I'd call us *stunned*, as in *so stunned our mouths actually hang open like fly traps*. We stare at our principal. Someone coughs.

"Certainly Ms. Bryce has taught you all about the history of our wonderful town?" asks Principal Klein.

She's never mentioned a word about the history of Liberty Falls, not even by accident. But no one says anything.

"You all know how the town got its name, right?" asks our

principal. He looks right at me, as if he expects me to blurt out the answer.

I put my finger under my collar. How did it get so hot in here suddenly? I look down and say to my notebook, "Because there used to be some sort of waterfall? And because liberty never falls, so it's sort of ironic, maybe?"

"So you *have* learned!" Principal Klein throws out a broad smile. "Anyway, don't forget to bring your signed permission slips before you get on the bus. Tell Ms. Bryce that Mrs. Frank will come by to collect them tomorrow morning."

A moment later, he's gone. The door is closed and no one in class dares to even breathe. But then Madelyn breaks the *so stunned our mouths actually hang open like fly traps* silence by asking the question on my lips. It's the question on all of our lips. "How are we going to go on a field trip without a teacher?"

We all groan in unison.

"It's over! I knew we'd be caught!" wails Maggie. "First the play, and now this!" She buries her face in her hands.

"Maybe we can just call the office and tell them Ms. Bryce is sick," suggests Madelyn. "And then they'll assign us a substitute for the day."

Maggie looks up, hopeful.

"No way," says Emmy. "Do you remember the *last* sub we had? Remember Drill Sergeant DeWitt? She made us do push-ups and run laps. She had a whistle around her neck, and whenever you answered a question wrong, she blew that whistle until your ears fell off. And then she made the entire class do fifty sit-ups."

We all remember Mrs. DeWitt. How could we forget? I still have nightmares about her.

Cooper shivers more than the rest of us. After seeing him sneak a candy bar bite, Mrs. DeWitt made Cooper run three laps around the school. And it was raining.

Cooper puts the chocolate bar he's holding into his backpack, as if Mrs. DeWitt is peering inside some magical faraway crystal ball, watching him snack.

No one wants Mrs. DeWitt back for even one day. And what if she stayed for two or three days? What if she became our *permanent* teacher?

There are continued moans across the class.

"My mom could take us," Jasmine suggests. "She loves museums."

"But won't she wonder where our real teacher is?" asks Eli.

"It's too risky," says Madelyn, and we all nod in agreement. "They would discover our secret, for sure."

Our incredible secret is unraveling like a giant ball of rolling yarn swatted by a determined kitty.

"If anyone finds out, then you're all sock haters, which means you smell like a sock or whatever!" yells Brian. "I don't want to repeat fifth grade."

"The Class That Repeated Fifth Grade." Maybe that'll be the next story I write. It'll be about a class that has to repeat the same grade over and over and over again until they are all one hundred and four years old.

In my story, the teacher doesn't age, though. So at the end, she's the student and the students are all her teachers.

"Maybe we can keep our secret and still go on the field trip," says Samantha. "I know an adult who will help us out and won't ask any questions. He'll pretend to be our teacher and everything."

I turn my head and stare at Samantha. I wait for her to laugh and tell us that she's kidding—that even her daddy can't save us from this mess. But she sits there calmly.

"Are you *sure?*" asks Maggie.

"Pretty sure," says Samantha. She nods her head energetically. "Very sure. Our secret will be safe with him."

"Then that's what we'll do," says Maggie.

No one else seems to have any other ideas, so we all agree that Samantha will supply a pretend teacher. Maggie immediately starts digging through Ms. Bryce's desk. I figure she must be looking for the permission slips.

I have to admit that Samantha surprises me. I thought I already knew everyone in class. But I guess you really need to get to know someone well before you really know someone well. And maybe you can't get to know someone just by watching that person from your desk.

23

SAMANTHA

I have a job to do, and the entire class is depending on me.

Me. Samantha O'Day.

No one has really depended on me for something before. Daddy usually pays people so we can depend on *them*.

It's a scary feeling. But it's sort of a nice feeling, too.

People say that money can't buy everything. You never hear rich people saying that.

Still, maybe there's something to it.

Mr. Wolcott sits in his lawn chair in front of the Old-Timers' Joint. (That's not my best name for the place, I admit. I'm distracted by all these good-deed thoughts.) He's wearing the same brown three-piece suit and wide, striped ascot he always wears.

I hang back. I'm a little nervous to ask him for a favor. What if he says no to me? Then what happens?

That's the problem with having lots of people depend on

you. You might have to let them down, even if you try your hardest.

I'm surprised that I care so much about helping out. Usually I don't think about the other kids in class at all. But now I find myself really, really, really wanting to help them.

"Franny!" Mr. Wolcott shouts, pulling me out of my deep thoughts. "In black ink my love may still shine bright!"

"Uh, right," I say, coming closer. I have no idea what that means, as usual. "My name is Samantha, remember?"

"Of course, of course. Have I told you of my one true love, Franny Bree? She was as lovely as a spring meadow, a delicate bloom on a hill of luscious green."

"Yeah, I know," I say. "Her bounty is as bouncy as the sea. Or you are the boundless sea. Or something like that." I need to get to the point. "Mr. Wolcott, I need a favor."

"A favor?" he repeats, his index finger caressing his chin. His eyebrows lift. He stands up, places one hand on his heart, and stretches out the other arm, as if addressing a queen.

His eyes had a sad look the other day, but I don't see any of that now. They glimmer, full of life. I wish my eyes twinkled like that. Fashion magazines don't tell you how to get your eyes to light up.

"Being your slave, what should I do but tend upon the hours and times of your desire? I have no precious time at all to spend, nor services to do, till you require," he says.

I'm not sure, but I think he's offering to help. Excellent. I might not be someone who gets invited to birthday parties, but I won't be someone who lets everyone down. "We've got a problem at school. We're going on a class trip, and we need an adult to go with us. You'll have to pretend you're our teacher."

"Pretend? Like acting in a play?"

"Exactly."

"It's been so long since I have acted in front of an audience." He says this quietly, to himself. I worry that he won't agree to help us. Then what? I feel antsy, and I keep myself from tapping my foot impatiently.

I suppose that's why good deeds feel good. Because they feel horrible when you don't know if they'll succeed.

Mr. Wolcott clears his throat, and when he speaks, he speaks louder and gestures, his arms sweeping with enthusiasm. "Yes! I shall do it! For all the world's a stage and all the men and women merely players." Then he smiles, a bright smile with white, gleaming, and nearly perfect teeth. His eyes twinkle so brightly I have to look away.

I grin as widely as he does.

I really don't think anything feels better than having a good deed get done. Not even buying shoes.

"But an actor needs his props!" exclaims Mr. Wolcott, whirling around in a circle, his arms swirling up, down, and around. "Costumes! Makeup! Should I wear a fake mustache or long, flowing wig? How about a top hat and tails? A walking cane? Perhaps I could go as the Prince of Demark, old Hamlet himself."

"I was thinking you could just act like a teacher."

Mr. Wolcott pumps his fist. "A splendid idea. Why, this will be the greatest role of my life! Still, I'll need a name. A character without a name is like a play without an act."

"Pick whatever name you want."

"How about Macbeth, Thane of Glamis!"

"Um, maybe you want to work on that?" I suggest.

He nods. "Perhaps."

"But thank you! Thank you for helping us!" He could call himself anything and I'd be super-excited. Well, he could call himself almost anything. I want to give him a giant, grateful hug, but instead I pat him on the shoulder. We work out all the other details, and I bid him farewell. I actually say, "I bid thee farewell."

Talking to Mr. Wolcott for a while will make you speak like that.

As I wave good-bye and head toward my building, all I can think is: *I did it!* I found our pretend teacher. Me! Samantha! And Daddy had nothing to do with it.

Winter break starts next week, and we're going to Hawaii. It's been over a year since we were last there, which seems like forever. The warm tropical sun will feel great, but I doubt it will make me feel any warmer than I do now.

I'm walking on a ray of sunshine, even though it's a cold and cloudy day.

Our doorman George smiles at me and I scurry past him into the lobby. "Welcome home, Miss Samantha."

"Fare thee well, George!" I say as I rush past, and then bite my tongue, trying to shake the Mr. Wolcott sayings from my mouth.

I head straight to the elevators. I need to change clothes for dance class and I'm running late. Mrs. Flatly, our teacher, said that we might start our dance for the end-of-year recital today. She'll likely pick parts right after winter break.

Last year, Penelope Poppers was the lead dancer in our class recital. She's the best dancer, sure, but I've been practicing really hard. Maybe I'll get a solo this year. If not, I'm sure Daddy can help fix that.

Doing things by yourself feels great, but sometimes you still need your parents to take care of things for you. It's a lot easier, anyway.

24

ERIC

I hand my parent permission slip to Lacey, who collects them for the class trip. My mom's name is scrawled on the bottom.

When I asked Mom for a signature last night, her face turned red and she glared at the slip. "The night before? What sort of school are they running? I'm calling your teacher. This is unacceptable."

I made up a story about how Ms. Bryce's phone is broken and that she also has laryngitis and we didn't have permission slips earlier because the school printer blew up.

It wasn't my best story, but it did the job. Mom signed the slip.

I didn't think it would matter, anyway. I figured Samantha wouldn't find a substitute teacher and then our secret wouldn't be a secret anymore.

But what do you know? I was wrong. Samantha brought an adult, just like she promised. He's old and wispy thin. He says his name is Mr. Chips, but I don't think that's his real name. He's wearing a brown tweed jacket with patches on the elbows, a pink bow tie, and a monocle in his left eye.

I've never seen a monocle up close before. He looks like an English professor from some old movie. He removes his eyewear and holds it up, admiring it. His voice booms, as if he's talking over a loud crowd, although no one else is talking. "All teachers need monocles, don't you agree? Doesn't it make me look academic?"

"Um, not really?" says Samantha.

Mr. Chips shrugs and puts the monocle in his inside jacket pocket.

He's full of energy. He waves his arms as if he's performing onstage while saying odd things like, "Though this be madness, yet there is method in't!" I think he's quoting Shakespeare. I recognize one or two lines from *Hamlet*, the play that I'm trying to read. But Shakespeare's words don't make any more sense to me when I hear them than when I read them.

Mr. Chips starts talking about how he's some great actor and about some old actress he used to love, but it's confusing. All of us in class keep nodding our heads and throwing him pretend smiles.

Samantha looks like she wants to hide under a desk. If we get through today, it will be a miracle.

Finally, there's a knock on the door. Mrs. Frank, the school secretary, enters the room and tells us that our bus is waiting for us to board it.

She waves to Adam and asks, "Have you eaten any homework or detention slips today?"

Adam shakes his head, blushes, and says, "Not yet." I have no idea what they are talking about.

Mrs. Frank collects the permission slips from Lacey, counting them out, and then, satisfied, leads us out the door. We follow her, single file, down the hallway and to the bus that's parked outside.

I'm last in line and Mr. Chips is at the front, but I can hear him clearly. He rambles on and on during the entire walk with a long monologue that begins, "To be, or not to be: that is the question."

I recognize the quote. It's a famous speech from *Hamlet*.

Finally, we exit the school doors. The bus is waiting right out front for us, with its motor running. As we gather around the doors to go inside, a deep voice calls from behind us. "Wait!"

It's Principal Klein.

We were so close to getting on the bus, too! But seeing our principal standing next to me reminds me of how much trouble we can get into for keeping this humongous secret.

This is going to be very bad.

Principal Klein approaches Mr. Chips. Our principal is a big man, and next to the ultra-thin Mr. Chips, he looks like a balloon. "Who are you?" he asks our pretend teacher, his big hands rubbing against his chin.

Samantha is next to them. Before Mr. Chips can answer the principal's question, Samantha says, "That's Mr. Chips. Our, uh, chaperone."

Principal Klein scans our group. "Ummm. But where's Ms. Bryce?"

Without missing a beat, the entire class answers, "The bathroom."

Principal Klein hesitates for a moment. His brow furrows. I think he's about to accuse our entire class of keeping a secret and that Mr. Chips is a fake.

But then our phony teacher rests his hand on Principal Klein's shoulder and says, "Dear sir, do not worry. I, Mr. Chips, teacher extraordinaire, am honored to shepherd these sheep. O! this learning, what a thing it is. What responsibility to captivate their minds! And . . . and . . ."

"Yes?" asks Principal Klein.

Mr. Chips looks at Samantha. "Um, um . . ." Then he whispers to her, "Line, please."

"Just tell him you're in charge until Ms. Bryce gets back," Samantha whispers back, just loud enough for me to hear.

"And I'm in charge!" exclaims Mr. Chips to our principal. As he says this, he removes the monocle from his pocket, puts it to his eye, and peers at our principal. "See? Don't I look academic?"

Samantha's face turns bright red. But Mr. Chips merely smiles. There's a moment of hesitation from our principal, a moment where I am convinced we're busted. But then our principal pats Mr. Chips on the back and says, "Great! Thanks for helping today. Have a wonderful trip."

He turns around and heads back into school.

And that's that.

My feet are still quivering as the bus doors open and we march up the steps. But I look at Mr. Chips. He *is* a great actor. I may not have followed half of what he was saying, but he almost had me convinced he was a real teacher, too.

I'm the last in line for the bus. I sit by myself in the empty front seat right behind the bus driver. I take a deep breath, anxious for the bus to start moving.

"Are we all here?" asks the driver. He doesn't know Mr. Chips isn't our regular teacher.

"Yes, we are," says Samantha.

"Then exit, stage left!" Mr. Chips declares.

And we're off!

25
KYLE

We're walking to the next museum exhibit when Brian yells to me, "Last one to the drinking fountain is a rotten egg!"

I'm no rotten egg, that's for sure. I don't even like regular eggs, unless you're throwing them at someone.

I think:

Some eggs are hard and others are runny.

But throw an egg at a head? That's pretty funny.

Brian gets a big lead to the fountain because he starts running before he even finishes saying "egg," which is cheating. But I'm way faster than him or Seth.

Seth gets off to a poor start, so he's got "rotten egg" written all over him.

I almost smack into an old lady who's walking in the hallway—"Excuse me!" she snaps—but I sidestep her just before we collide. I skid slightly on the floor but overtake Brian at the wire, reaching the water fountain one arm length in front. "I smell rotten eggs," I say, and then take a long winner's sip from the spout.

Seth arrives last. I keep my finger on the fountain button so the water keeps spraying, and slap my palm against it.

Water splashes onto Seth and Brian, a big wave on their shirts, and a little puddle lands on the pants of an old guy standing next to us. "Watch it!" he huffs at me.

"Sorry," I say with a giggle.

A few other adults glare at us in the hallway.

Still, this is the best field trip ever. No teacher. No rules. We can run in the halls.

The rest of our class is already looking at the Native American exhibit, and we join them. Inside the room, glass displays feature Native Americans wearing long feathery headdresses and tan shirts with bright red and green patterns around the shoulders. On the wall hangs a painting of an entire caravan of Native Americans hunting buffalo. An old canoe dangles from the ceiling.

A sign next to me describes how people lived back in the early 1400s, way before English settlers came to the area. I lean over to read it.

"Boring!" Brian burps out from behind me.

I open my mouth and push out a burp of my own. It's not as loud as Brian's, but for an on-the-spot, unprepared burp, it's not half bad.

"Listen to me!" says Seth. His burp rumbles for ten seconds, easy. We crack up.

"Knock it off," says Paige, who is standing near us with Lacey and Maggie. She folds her arms and glares at us with disapproval etched into her pursed lips. "You guys should grow up and try learning something. You sound like burping moose. You can't be ignorant bullies your whole lives, you know."

"I know stuff!" I retort as Paige shakes her head.

The three girls glare at us and I frown back at them. Sure, I don't get grades like they get, but that doesn't mean I don't know stuff. Books and school things aren't the only things worth knowing. For example, it takes real talent to burp well. You have to swallow a bunch of air, open your airway, and then let it out quickly. Not everyone can do that.

And I wrote a play. I make up rhymes. That takes talent, too.

I'm not just an ignorant bully or a burping moose.
Don't worry—you can count on me!
I'm a new Kyle! Just wait and see.

The girls stomp away as Brian burps again, short and quiet. Seth laughs, but I don't. Burping doesn't seem so funny anymore.

This exhibit is actually interesting. I turn my back on the burping-moose boys and try to focus on it. Right next to us, a glass case is filled with all sorts of arrowheads, and over in the corner sits a tepee. I hear Seth burp behind me and snicker.

Paige, Lacey, and Maggie stomp straight toward Mr. Chips, who stands with Samantha and Giovanna. As the girls talk to him, Paige points at us with stabbing, angry gestures.

I bet she's telling him we're ignorant.

Mr. Chips answers her in a loud, booming voice. It's even louder than Brian's burps, so I can hear it clearly, even across the room. "Love all, trust a few, do wrong to none!"

I have no idea what he's talking about.

Brian burps. Seth laughs.

There are plenty of other people in the exhibit room, too. Some stare at Mr. Chips, and some glare at us. Brian burps again.

"Knock it off," I say.

"What's gotten into you?" snaps Brian.

"Nothing." I read the exhibit sign next to me.

Brian burps, but I ignore him.

"Let's go to the next room," says Seth.

I'm not ready to go, though. I haven't finished looking at the exhibits in *this* room. There's a display across the room showing a bunch of people dancing around a fire, their faces covered in paint. It looks interesting.

"I bet we could make a break for it," Brian whispers to me. "The old dude wouldn't even notice."

"Last one to the cafeteria is a rotten egg!" says Seth.

"Knock it off, guys," I grumble. "You're acting like ignorant moose."

Someone shouts, and it's not Brian or Seth doing the yelling, either. It's Mr. Chips again. Now he's arguing with a security guard. Samantha and Eric are with them. I wonder what's going on.

"Thou lump of foul deformity!" Mr. Chips says loudly. "The tartness of your face sours ripe grapes. I denounce you, sir."

I have no idea what Mr. Chips is talking about, but he's angry and he looks like he wants to punch the guard.

Yow. Yow. Yow.

26
SAMANTHA

Well, this is the last time I'm doing a good deed, that's for sure.

Now I know why I never do them. What a disaster of a day!

This morning, Mr. Wolcott waited for me outside the Big House for Old Geezers (that's a name that makes me smile) wearing a bright pink bow tie and with a monocle in his eye, like the Monopoly guy wears. "Call me Mr. Chips!" he said in a loud British accent.

All things considered, the name could have been worse. I told him he was doing my class a big favor. I was grateful. Sincerely.

And when I got to school and introduced "Mr. Chips," the other kids were really impressed that I had saved the day. Giovanna said that I was fantastically awesome, and that made me feel even more fantastically awesome.

But then he kept on quoting things like he always does. "You're supposed to be a teacher," I reminded him.

"And what life lessons we learn from the great bard, Shakespeare himself!" said Mr. Chips, who then added, "We know what we are, but know not what we may be."

"Uh, okay," I said, biting my lip.

But even with him quoting things like usual, we arrived at the museum and everything was going well. Mr. Wolcott had been in a wonderful mood. He probably didn't go on trips away from the Big House for Old Geezers (my name for the day) very often. We had been in the museum for about an hour and were in the Native American exhibit admiring their moccasins. I was trying to explain to Giovanna why shoes are the most important fashion accessory and how color coordination was not optional. I think I was finally starting to get through to her.

But then my shoulder was tapped.

"I think something's wrong with Mr. Chips," said Eric.

"Who?" I asked.

"Mr. Chips. Our pretend teacher."

I thought he was next to me. I had been keeping Mr. Wolcott by my side all morning.

He stood in the middle of the room, his hands balled into fists. He breathed heavily. I quickly walked over to him. "Are you okay, Mr. Chips?"

"Him!" Mr. Wolcott pointed to a tall, scrawny security guard against the far wall. The guard was an old guy, in his sixties at least.

"Do you need help?" Maybe Mr. Wolcott had some sort of emergency and needed to alert the authorities for assistance. "What can I do?" I asked, genuinely concerned. Maybe we needed to find a doctor.

"That man is Jeffrey Barrows," Mr. Wolcott announced, still staring at the guard. "My archenemy!"

The guard yawned. He didn't notice Mr. Wolcott pointing at him with a long, crooked finger or the angry glare in our chaperone's eyes.

"That's just a security guard," I said. The scrawny old guy across the room didn't look like he could hurt a fly. Still, Mr. Wolcott seemed pretty worked up.

"I would recognize him anywhere!" Mr. Wolcott declared. His nostrils flared. He took a step forward, toward the guard.

I stepped in the path of Mr. Wolcott to block his way. He tried to sidestep me, but I moved in front of him again. "Let me pass," he demanded.

"I think you might be mistaken, *Mr. Chips.*" I hoped if I said his teacher name, it might remind him he was supposed to be acting, and that teachers didn't start fights with security guards. But I don't think he even heard me. His stare never left the guard. A few people were watching us now. I turned my back to them.

"Have I told you about the love of my life, Franny Bree?" he asked.

I assured him that I might have heard her name once or twice.

"It was fifty years ago. Franny and I were set to perform on the London stage. It would be a grand performance of *Romeo and Juliet*. We would tour Europe, playing the star-crossed lovers. If not for *him*!"

His nostrils flared. His heels bounced. His face was tomato red. Mr. Wolcott was always so sweet on his lawn chair. I had never seen this side of him.

"I planned to propose marriage," he proclaimed. "Our happiness was assured. But the night before we were set to leave, I fell ill. Barrow went to London in my place. He stole her heart. I never saw Franny again."

"I'm so sorry." I pictured Mr. Wolcott sitting on his lawn chair when I came home from school every day. I'd never seen him with friends or family. Did he have any? Maybe he'd spent half his life regretting his lost love. "But you can't blame someone else because you got sick."

"The cad poisoned me!" shouted Mr. Wolcott. "True, I cannot prove it—but I know it with every fiber of my soul. He wanted me out of the way so he could take my Franny from me." He averted his gaze from the guard and looked down at me. I have never seen eyes so sad.

I wanted to give him a big hug, but that would have been totally weird.

Mr. Wolcott looked away for a moment, wiping a tear from his eye. But then, when he turned back around, his expression of despair was gone and once again replaced with anger. His body seemed to vibrate with rage. He stared at the guard and shook his fist. "Revenge will be mine!"

"But are you really, really sure that's him?" I asked. "It's been a long time." I patted Mr. Wolcott on the shoulder to help calm him down. He had been speaking so loudly that everyone in the room now stared at us. I threw some of the gawkers a soft smile to assure them nothing was wrong.

I shouldn't have glanced away, because Mr. Wolcott quickly stepped around me. He marched toward the guard.

"Wait! Come back!" I begged as he stomped across the room. I hurried after him.

As he drew closer to the guard, Mr. Wolcott's face grew fiercer and fiercer.

"So, Barrows! At last we meet!" Mr. Wolcott barked between clenched teeth. He puffed out his chest and glared up at the guard, who was a few inches taller than our pretend teacher.

The guard threw Mr. Wolcott a puzzled expression. "Excuse me?"

The guard was even older than he had looked across the room. He must have been in his seventies, at least. I pointed to his name tag. "Look! His name is Clyde. So he can't be Jeffrey Barrows. It's a different guy."

But Mr. Wolcott waved me away. "Names are easily changed." I pulled Mr. Wolcott's arm to lead him away, but he wasn't budging. "Thou art a Castilian King urinal!" Mr. Wolcott shouted at the guard. The veins in his neck throbbed and his lips shook. "Thou hast no more brain than I have in mine elbows!"

"Please, you're going to ruin everything," I pleaded to Mr. Wolcott.

I had no idea what our pretend teacher was talking about, but it was obviously meant to be insulting.

Our class secret would be exposed. Everyone would blame me.

I wondered what Daddy would say when I ended up in jail and needed him to bail me out.

Good deeds are a lot more trouble than they're worth.

"You scullion. You rampallian. You fustilarian. I'll tickle your catastrophe!" ranted our half-crazy teacher impersonator, his eyes bulging.

The guard had obviously had enough. He held a walkie-talkie, and he raised it to his mouth. I was certain that he was going to call for backup, and then a bunch of guys would run into the room and tackle Mr. Wolcott.

I hoped jail was comfortable.

But then a funny thing happened. The guard released the button. His eyes grew wider and he lowered his speaker. He stared at Mr. Wolcott. "Hey! I recognized that. You're quoting Shakespeare, right? Was that line from Shakespeare's play *King Lear*? I read it once, but that was a long, long time ago. I was a theater major back in the day."

Something seemed to click just then. Mr. Wolcott's face relaxed. The wrinkles of rage seemed to disappear. His anger just sort of melted away, like an ice-cream sundae you've left on the balcony of your high-rise penthouse. He unclenched his fists. He coughed. He smiled. "Actually, that line was from his play *Henry the Fourth, Part Two*. I performed it in my youth."

"I did regional theater back home in Kentucky, but nothing too significant," said the guard. I now noticed he had a very slight Southern accent. "Were you an actor?"

"I *am* an actor," Mr. Wolcott corrected him. He seemed to grow taller. He lifted his chin. He laughed. He was a completely different person from the madman I saw an instant ago. He was himself again. He looked down at me, laughed, and said to the guard, "I mean, I'm a teacher of course." Then, he put on his monocle and gazed at the guard with a wry eyebrow lift. "See?"

The guard nodded. "Ah. Yes, indeed. Very academic."

Mr. Wolcott nodded. "I know."

A few seconds later we were walking away. Mr. Wolcott smiled. "A good man, that," he said.

"I thought he was your archenemy?" I asked.

"Him? No. Barrows would never mistake *Henry the Fourth* for *King Lear*. Those two plays weren't even written in the same decade."

I was too relieved to say anything else. I just nodded. "Let's look at the exhibits," I suggested, pointing to a glass display of Native American fur clothing and eager to get his mind on something else. Meanwhile, my heart beat a million miles a minute. It's still beating just as fast now.

The rest of the trip went without a hitch, thankfully. Still, it was way too stressful.

"I was resplendent today, wasn't I?" asks Mr. Wolcott as we walk home from school together.

I'm not sure what *resplendent* means. If it means *I was a pain in the neck and almost ruined everything*, then yes, he was very, very resplendent.

"If only the esteemed Franny Bree had seen me," he says. "She would have marveled at my performance."

Mr. Wolcott always rattles on about meaningless stuff, but maybe much of it isn't meaningless to him. "You really loved her, didn't you?"

He nods. "Loved? Past tense? Oh, love never extinguishes completely. Not true love, anyway." That twinkle in his eye dims for a moment, but then it quickly rekindles. He laughs, and then he's the same Mr. Wolcott I see on his lawn chair every day.

He waves good-bye and turns down the entranceway to the Home for Really Old and Sometimes Baffling Guys and Gals.

"Thank you for coming today!" I shout after him. And, despite everything, I actually mean it. Mostly.

27
KYLE

An eraser bounces off the back of my head. "Two points!" yells Brian.

"Quit it. I'm not playing," I grunt.

Brian shrugs and hurls an eraser at Seth, who ducks behind his chair.

They're just ignorant.

Brian burps.

They're just ignorant burping moose.

I ignore them and think of yesterday. I look around the class. I still can't believe we made it through the entire field trip without being caught.

Yow. Yow. Yow.

But not everyone is celebrating our success. Maggie runs around in a panic and yanks her hair. "We need to practice the play! We are not prepared! Friday is in two days!" she shouts.

No one pays much attention to her. But she's right. If we don't practice, our performance will stink.

I want to impress our parents Friday night. I want to impress my mom, most of all.

I don't think I've ever spent so much time on a homework project before. I've been spending a lot of time revising and editing the play, even at home.

Not that this is homework, because I assigned it to myself.

No, I think it counts as homework. It *should* count as homework, anyway.

The crowd applauds as we act and sing—
Maybe I could get used to this homework thing.

I'm especially proud of the songs. Everyone loves a musical.

But instead of rehearsing, Adam and Lizzie doodle on the floor. Danny and Gavin play paper football. Cooper eats a candy bar.

I whistle. Loudly. Everyone looks at me. "Maggie says we need to practice the play," I snap.

Maggie throws me a grateful smile. Adam and Lizzie stop doodling and join her, and so do all the other actors. Behind me, Giovanna and Samantha remove a roll of large brown paper from our supply closet to start the set decorations.

Brian and Seth continue to hurl erasers at each other and burp.

Don't they get sick of goofing off?

I think about last night. Mom was busy changing AJ's diaper, and she asked me to take the meat loaf out of the oven. I told her I would in a moment, and I was planning to do it at the next commercial break, except I forgot.

Mom was pretty steamed, although she was not as steamy as the burnt meat loaf, which Mom made us eat even though it was charred and black. Marley and Nate wouldn't talk to me the rest of the night.

Later, I asked Mom about the promotion and she said she was turning it down. I begged her to reconsider. I told her I'd hold down the fort.

She told me that she didn't want the promotion and it had nothing to do with me.

I don't believe her.

I haven't told her I wrote the class play. I want to surprise her. Maybe, if the play is absolutely fantastic, she'll see that she can depend on me.

I'll prove to her that I'm good for something. I'll prove that to everyone.

A flying eraser grazes my hair. "I said I'm not playing," I grumble to Seth.

"You're no fun anymore," says Brian.

I ignore him and join the actors. As the playwright, I need to be prepared to make more script changes and help the director.

I should write a part for our hamster, Soda. Soda can play the part of George Washington's dog. I think he had a lot of dogs.

Wait. Soda! I forgot to feed him this morning. That's my job.

How am I supposed to take care of my brothers and sisters if I can't even remember to feed a hamster?

I hurry to Soda's cage to fill his food bowl with hamster food pellets and to refill his water bottle.

The top of the cage is open. That's strange.

"How are you doing, Soda?" I ask with a smile.

But when I look inside, Soda is missing.

"Hey! Who has Soda?" I ask loudly, scanning the room.

No one says a word. Everyone stares at me. I point at the cage. "Soda is gone. Who has him?"

I'm met with silence and blank stares.

"Who was the last person to go in his cage?" I ask.

I'm met with more silence. More stares.

I fed him yesterday before the field trip. I remember, because I lifted him from the cage, stroked his fur, and pretended to throw him at Emmy and then Jasmine.

They fall for that joke every time, screaming and cringing. It was funny. It's always funny.

After that, I put Soda down on the floor while I poured some food into his dish. Then I put Soda back, right? Then I closed the door, right?

Or did I start playing Eraser Wars?

"You've lost our hamster?" Jade sounds very angry. She glares at me.

"No, of course not," I say. I mean, I couldn't have lost Soda, right?

I'm not *that* completely worthless, am I?

My stomach starts twitching with worry. My mouth fills with spit, like I'm going to get sick. I duck down to look under the desk, but there's no Soda hiding there. "Help me find him!" I shout. My voice fills with panic.

"Soda's a girl," says Ryan.

"Then help me find *her!*" I shout, louder.

But, really? Soda is a girl?

Everyone in class stops what they were doing to crawl around the floor, checking under desks and in the corners. Even Brian and Seth quit throwing erasers to join the search.

Maggie looks in the teacher's desk, opening drawers as if our hamster suddenly acquired the magical power of opening and hiding in drawers. But I suppose we need to check every inch of the room.

Cooper looks in the supply cabinet. I check the bookshelf. Nothing.

Soda is gone. Vanished. And it's all my fault.

I really am good for nothing.

28

SAMANTHA

I can't believe Soda is gone. Our pet rat! Missing!

Or hamster. Or whatever it was.

I always try to ignore the rodent. I touched it once, because Ms. Bryce passed it around class on the first day of school. Everyone had to hold the creature and pet it.

I rested it in my hand. I stroked its fur.

And it peed. Right. On. My. Hand.

I screamed. It was awful. I washed and washed and washed, yet my hand still smelled like rodent pee all day. I vowed never to get near it again.

Who thought that keeping a live rodent in a classroom was a good idea, anyway?

The mere thought of a rodent in our penthouse apartment gives me the shivers.

And now, thinking of that creature lurking somewhere in the room, hiding in the shadows or in my desk, is a terrifying picture that I need to get out of my head. I bet I'll have night-mares tonight.

What if it pees on me again?

I peek in my desk. Thankfully, it's not there. But still! It could run up my pants or something.

That's it. I'm only wearing boots to school from now on. I'll order a new pair or three tonight.

The other kids in class seem really upset about Soda missing, though. Kyle looks like he's going to cry, which is something I never imagined I'd see.

I could ask Daddy to buy a new hamster for the class—a hamster that's specially trained not to run away, has hypo-allergenic fur, and only goes to the bathroom on command.

But maybe, just maybe, buying a new Soda wouldn't be as awesome as actually finding the old Soda. My legs would still be in danger of a rodent crawling up them.

Most important, everyone would still be upset.

I thought when Ms. Bryce quit, things were going to be perfect. I really did. I could read magazines and help the girls in the class with fashion advice. I'd have less homework, which would mean more time for online shoe shopping. I wouldn't have to worry about being yelled at in class.

But things aren't working out anything like I thought they would. One bad thing happens after another. And I care about it much, much, much more than I would have ever thought.

Maybe we're just not ready for a teacherless class.

I mean, take a look at poor Maggie. She's exhausted grading homework, giving assignments, and directing our play. I never want to work that hard at anything.

I'm glad I'm not Maggie, that's for sure.

Brian and Seth high-five each other. Kyle yells his silly "Yow! Yow!" thing. They found Soda under the teacher's desk! What a relief—wearing boots every day would be so monotonous.

No . . . wait. Never mind. Kyle frowns again. That wasn't Soda under the desk at all. It was an enormous dust ball. Brian just blew the ball at Gavin and it clings to his cheek. Yuck. Don't they clean these rooms, like, ever?

Our weekly housekeepers would never allow dust bunnies and dirt clods in our penthouse apartment. Aunt Karen wouldn't stand for it.

She might not always make the best eggs or lemonade or remember to cut the toast diagonally, but she is a big help. I'm glad she's living with us. Maybe I should tell her that sometime.

After all, I'll need her help keeping my boots shiny and polished if we don't find that rodent soon.

"Samantha?" It's Emmy and she's shuffling over to me slowly. Her jeans are too baggy and she cuffs them at the bottom. Those are two basic jean *do not do*s. I don't say anything, though, because I'm realizing that people don't want to hear that sort of stuff even if it's for their own good. Besides, I'm looking at the card in her hand, which she holds up. "It was pretty great that you invited Mr. Chips to be our teacher yesterday," she says.

"It was nothing. He was glad to help." I'm grateful that Emmy doesn't mention the screaming match he had with the security guard and all his strange quotes.

Emmy hands me her card. "I'm having a party at my house this weekend. I hope you can come. Um, I forgot to give one to you the other day." I thank her for the invitation, and she walks back to her friends. I turn the card over in my hand. I know it's only a piece of paper, and it's only a party with a bunch of girls I'm not even friends with, but I place the card inside my notebook, careful not to bend the corners. Then I walk over to the other kids and start to help look for our missing hamster, smiling more than I can remember smiling in a long, long time.

29
MAGGIE

Soda is missing and it's just another nail in my rotting wooden coffin. It's just one more excuse for Harvard to laugh at me. It's just one more reason why my future is doomed.

But I don't have time to worry about our missing hamster. I don't even have time to worry about poor, miserable me. Not now. Not with a class to lead and a play to direct.

Of all the lousy things happening, of all the problems staring at us, the school play is the biggest worry of them all.

"Are you okay?" Lacey asks. She stands next to me, a look of genuine concern on her face.

"Why wouldn't I be fine?" I answer, lifting my chin.

But I'm not fine, no, not at all. The actors don't know their lines, and they don't seem to care. Adam and Lizzie are too busy staring at each other to pay attention. Gavin, who plays John Hancock, has one line—one crummy line—and he can't even remember it.

Trevor, our Paul Revere, keeps yelling, "The British are here! The British are here!"

"No, they're coming!" I yell. "The British are *coming*!"

"They are? Where?" he asks.

"No! That's your line!"

"Well, I think 'The British are here' is a way better line than shouting that they are just *coming*," he says. "Sometimes my grandparents say they are coming over for lunch, and they don't show up until dinnertime."

I just throw up my arms and scream. Sometimes screaming makes you feel better, but not in this case. All it does is hurt my throat.

This morning, I thought I found a gray hair in my bed. A gray hair! I'm ten years old. Ten-year-olds don't have gray hair. Although, when I looked at it closer, I may have been wrong. The hair might have been a thread from my gray-and-white bedspread.

We're practicing the second act, and Cooper reads a line. Cooper, who plays Thomas Jefferson, actually knows most of his lines, and he has a lot of them. Which is great, except he just might be the most terrible actor to ever try to act. He's supposed to be passionate about freedom! American independence! Jefferson wrote the Declaration of Independence, after all. But Cooper sounds as soft and oozy as a marshmallow.

Thomas Jefferson was not a marshmallow. He was a leader. Like me.

"Put some heart into it!" I insist. "Can't you act?"

"I am acting. I'm acting great," says Cooper, who wouldn't know great acting if an Academy Award fell on his head.

"Just do it my way!" I recite his line exactly the way it should be recited, syllable by syllable. I am forceful in my delivery and passionate.

Then he repeats the line, and sounds like a marshmallow.

I don't know why I have to do everything myself.

At least he sings well. He has a lot of singing parts. Still, we're going to make complete fools of ourselves Friday night—that's in only two days!—and our secret will be discovered and we'll be ruined. I'll be ruined.

Samantha and Giovanna are supposed to be building sets, but every time I glance over to them, they're flipping through magazines.

I holler at them to get to work, and they look at me, eyes glazed, as if I'm speaking Latin.

I know quite a bit of Latin, but I wasn't speaking it.

But at least they're mostly quiet. Brian and Seth keep playing their stupid eraser game and shouting. I glare at them, but they just laugh. "Knock it off!" I finally yell. They ignore me.

Trevor and Gavin watch me and whisper something to each other. I can't hear them, but they probably think I'm being bossy again. I ignore them. Whatever.

Leaders need to be a *little* bossy. That's why they call them bosses!

Meanwhile, Kyle works on script changes. He's not acting like a blockhead, thankfully, but we're running out of time. Kyle has eliminated some of the more terribly inaccurate parts, such as the scene where George Washington hurls erasers at the British and wins the Eraser War, which made no sense at all. But his play still needs a lot of work.

"Ben Franklin did not have superpowers," I argue.

"But that's the best part," says Kyle with a frown.

I yawn. I was up all night creating today's assignment sheets. I don't have time to correct Kyle's mistakes. I rub my eyes and yawn again. Doesn't the class understand the sacrifice I'm making for them?

Being a teacher has been way harder than I ever imagined. I hate to admit it, but we could use Ms. Bryce right now. I picture her swooping through the window on a broomstick to take control. Since witches fly on broomsticks, that would be particularly appropriate.

So, maybe we don't want Ms. Bryce returning to teach our class. Not *her*. But we need *someone*. Better yet, maybe the entire Friday night event will be pushed back a month, or two. Or forever.

"Do you need any help preparing homework?" asks Paige, Lacey by her side. They ask this same question four times a day.

"We can totally help out," says Paige.

"I'm fine," I insist. "Splendid, magnificent, and exceptional, thank you."

But I'm doomed, doomed, doomed.

They turn away and I swallow the spittle that's forming in puddles inside my anguished mouth. Maybe they can help. Maybe leaders don't have to do *everything*.

Sometimes, a little help can be, well, helpful.

I'm about to speak up and call them back, but two door raps interrupt me. At first, I brighten. Maybe our Friday night event has been canceled! My wish came true, like in a fairy tale. We're saved.

But then my brain settles. Fairy tales don't come true. Two door raps equal our warning sign. The eraser throwers sit. I sit tall, my chin up.

Principal Klein enters the room. He scans the class. We're all seated, frozen smiles on our faces. "Where's Ms. Bryce?" he asks. Before anyone can respond, he shakes his head and says, "I know. The bathroom." He clears his throat. "I was just checking to ask how the play was coming along. I'm excited to see your performance Friday night. We're anticipating a big turnout from the community."

"It's going great," I answer, forcing an extra-wide grin to spread across my face.

I may be doomed, but I won't show my defeat. That's what leaders do.

30
ADAM

I don't want to pick the short pencil, really, truly. I try *not* to pick it. I study the eraser ends of the pencils. They all seem the same height. If one looks a little shorter, I purposely avoid that pencil. I remember where the short pencil lurked the last time I chose, and so I nab a pencil from a completely different location.

Yet here I go again, with the short pencil in my hand.

"Oh, come on!" I complain. I don't want to go. I need to stay and rehearse the play. I have the biggest part! I want to help look for Soda, too—we need everyone to search for her. All hands on deck! We shouldn't be sending kids to the principal's office now.

"Don't forget your detention slip," says Eli.

I growl at him.

When I arrive at the school office, Mrs. Frank shakes her head at me. She doesn't have to say, *You again? Really? Can't you behave?* but I know that's what she is thinking. She holds out her hand without saying a word, and I place my slip on her palm. She reads the note.

"You ate Lizzie's sneakers?" she asks.

I shrug.

"For heaven's sake, why?"

"I was in the mood for some fast food."

She groans and points to the empty row of chairs. "Take a seat."

31
ERIC

Maggie directs our class play, but honestly, I think she is in over her head. She keeps screaming at everyone, pulling her hair, and complaining that we're all blockheads.

Maybe I should talk to Maggie. I could show her the revisions I've made to the play. I've scribbled a few pages of notes, rewritten scenes, added some new ones, and eliminated others. I think I've made it a lot better.

A musical has three parts: the lyrics, the music, and the script. The script consists of all the parts that aren't sung. I can't fix the music or the lyrics, that's not what I'm good at, but I can improve the script a lot. I *have* improved the script a lot.

For example, the Boston Tea Party wasn't a tea party hosted by Martha Washington. So I took that scene out of the play. The Boston Tea Party was actually about a bunch of people throwing tea into Boston Harbor to protest taxes. I bet Kyle could write a good song about tea.

I also think we should completely eliminate scene number nine in the second act, in which Thomas Jefferson emails the Declaration of Independence to the British.

I don't think it happened like that.

But I doubt Maggie would listen to me, anyway. She would just get mad and tell me to mind my own business. Kyle would be mad, too.

I don't want to make trouble.

After all, I'm a colorless plant: unnoticed and unplucked.

So I keep my notes in my backpack, stay in my seat, and write a new story instead, a story that I can keep to myself. I call my new story "Soda, the Magical Disappearing Hamster." But Soda quickly becomes an invisible rabbit. Eric, the hero of the story, is a shy, quiet kid who captures a rabbit in a field. He doesn't realize he has actually captured a rabbit that can turn itself invisible. He arrives in class with a towel over a rabbit cage. All the kids in class gather around Eric as he removes the towel.

The cage is empty.

Confused, Eric opens the cage to look inside. The rabbit leaps out. It's invisible, so nobody can see the creature as it runs around biting students, knocking things over, and eating a box of cupcakes one of the students brought for a birthday treat.

No one knows what's happening until the rabbit briefly turns itself visible. Everyone yells at Eric to do something, so he lures the critter back into the cage with some lettuce from the turkey sandwich in his lunch bag.

Eric knew he shouldn't have shared anything with the class. He should have kept quiet.

After school, Eric takes the rabbit back to the field and opens the cage to return it to the wild. "Get out of here!" he yells.

As he stands there, cage open, Eric hears a loud bull snorting from behind him. He spins around, but the field is empty. Still, the snorting grows louder and Eric sees the long grass being crushed beneath mighty invisible bull feet, coming closer and closer and closer until—

"No! That's all wrong!" Maggie yells at Lizzie from the front of the classroom. I look up from my page. Adam, back from the principal's office, jumps in and argues with Maggie. Things aren't going very well. Maggie complains that the play is a complete mess.

"One if by sea," says Eli, who is playing Paul Revere.

"It's *two* if by sea!" yells Maggie. "Can't anyone do anything right?"

Eli stomps away. So do Lizzie and Adam. Maggie stands by herself, her eyes red and puffy. I think she might cry.

I sigh and remove my script notes from my backpack. Something needs to be done, and not just with the script— with everything. The sets need to be set better, the acting needs to be acted better, and the costumes need to be created somehow, too.

I can't do everything, but I can do my part. I take a deep breath. I consider approaching Maggie, but instead I turn around and slink toward Samantha, who is huddled with Giovanna in the back reading a magazine instead of creating the sets. I stop three times before I reach her. Each time I stop, I consider returning to my seat. But then I start walking again.

And then, somehow, I've crossed the room and am standing right next to Samantha. I didn't even realize I had walked so far.

She looks up at me. "What do *you* want?" she asks, as if accusing me of something.

I wish I could disappear, like an invisible rabbit. What was I thinking? She'll probably laugh at me. I should have kept my idea to myself. I should have remembered I'm a colorless plant. But it's too late now, so I clear my throat and unlock my arms, clasped in front of me. I take a deep breath. "Um, so, this play. It's sort of a disaster," I say.

Samantha nods. "I've noticed."

"Well, um, I have an idea, but I need your help."

"My help?" she says. A small smile creeps onto her lips. Her eyes lock onto mine. "I'm just the person to ask. I specialize in helping. What can I do?"

32
SAMANTHA

As I walk home from school, I can't stop feeling all worried inside, my body nervously tingling, head to toe.

The last time I felt this worried was last year, when this really cute pair of brown leather riding boots were out of stock at all the online stores and I didn't know when I would get them.

But this feels even more worrisome, and it's all about school. School has never bothered me before, either. I mean, sure, Ms. Bryce bothered me a little. But I would stop feeling bothered after the bell rang and I was home.

So why do I *feel* like everything matters a whole lot? Why do I care what happens? Why do I want everything to turn out for the best—not just for me, but for Emmy and Jade and everyone?

As I walk, I clutch Emmy's party invitation in my hand. I didn't want it to get crushed in my backpack. The paper is light blue colored, and it calms me.

In class, I'm supposed to design and build sets for the play, but working is hard and I chipped a nail. Everyone thinks I've been goofing off, reading my fashion magazines instead.

Nope.

I've been reading the script. I've got the whole thing practically memorized.

I like to imagine it's me on that stage, in the starring role. Me!

But I don't want anyone to know I'm reading the play. I have my reputation to consider, and besides, it would set a bad example for the other girls.

It's not fashionable to care.

"Top of the afternoon, Franny!" shouts Mr. Wolcott from his lawn chair.

I smile and walk over to his chair, holding tightly on to my invitation and remembering my conversation with Eric. I'm a little nervous, but I brush those concerns aside and return his big grin. I have a good deed to do. "I'm Samantha, remember?"

"Of course I know who you are! A rose by any other name would smell as sweet."

"Thanks, I think."

"Are you in need of Mr. Chips again?" he asks. "You know, the *Times* once called me 'a captivating, rising star of the stage'! Although their most lavish praise was for the impeccable Franny Bree, of course."

I look for a trace of sadness in his eyes as he mentions Franny Bree's name, but I don't see it. Not today, anyway. But then again, Mr. Wolcott is an exceptional actor.

"No, I don't need Mr. Chips," I say with a slight roll of my eyes. "But I have another favor to ask you."

He peers in closer. "Yes?"

"Mr. Chips can't help us this time. But you can."

33
MAGGIE

I have no appetite for dinner. Instead, my stomach gurgles in despair. I linger at the table while Mom and Dad sit in the study. Finally, I get up.

Dad is snug in the recliner, his thick reading glasses perched on the end of his nose as he peruses a book about Richard Nixon, a former president of the United States. Mom lies on the couch holding a mystery novel, her head resting on a sofa cushion. She licks her fingers before turning each page. It's a habit that I hate because it means her saliva is on every book. That's why I don't read the books Mom reads.

I much prefer science books, anyway.

I stand facing my parents, but they haven't noticed me yet. I clear my throat. Mom looks up. "Yes, honey?"

Her voice jolts Dad. He twitches, and then looks over at me, too. "Maggie?" he says, peering over his glasses. "Don't you have homework you should be doing?"

"The girl can take a break," Mom says to Dad. "Winter vacation starts soon, you know."

"Well, that's what I wanted to talk about," I say. My shoulders sag.

"What's wrong?" Mom puts down her book and leans forward, eyeing me closely. She can see the defeated look on my face. I don't try to hide it.

"We can still visit over break, but I don't think I want to go to college at Harvard," I say. I don't tell them why. I don't tell them that no school will want me after they learn what a teaching failure I am, and how my class lost both a room hamster and ruined a school play under my watch. I feel like a total blockhead.

"What are you talking about?" asks Dad. "Of course you're going to Harvard. It's not even a question."

"She's only in fifth grade," says Mom.

Dad frowns.

I've let him down. I know it. Every family has a failure, a black sheep, an absolute shameful embarrassment. And I'm ours.

I can't even look at my father. I can't stand to see the disappointment on his face.

Tears gather at the corners of my eyes, sobs choke in my throat, and I run upstairs to my room. I hate for them to see me cry. I, Maggie Cranberry, never cry. At least, not usually.

Closing the door behind me, I throw myself onto my bed.

The play is a disaster, our doom is certain, and the discovery of our secret is guaranteed. Now I understand why Ms. Bryce was so grouchy all the time, and so annoyed when kids failed to listen to her. Maybe she wasn't such a horrible teacher after all. Maybe if I taught school for a hundred years to roomfuls of ungrateful kids, I would be just like her.

Frankly, it's amazing she wasn't more cantankerous.

Cantankerous means grouchy, crabby, and mean, mean, mean.

There's a knock on my bedroom door. It's Mom's knock. Dad always knocks in threes, but Mom knocks softer and in two sets of two: two knocks, pause, and then two knocks. "Is everything okay?" she asks from the other side of my door. "Do you want to talk?"

"Everything is great!" I holler between my sobs.

"But what's wrong?"

I bury my head in my pillow to mask my crying. "Nothing!" I say. Nothing is wrong at all—other than my being a complete failure at the age of ten. I never thought I'd be such a disappointment.

"Okay. But if you want to talk, your dad and I will be downstairs," Mom replies.

At some point I fall asleep on my bed in a pillow puddle of tears. Deep in the night, I wake up from a horrible dream.

I was charging up a hill during the Revolutionary War. Kyle was there, and so were a bunch of other kids.

And we were all on the British side.

34
KYLE

"Do I actually have to wear these wooden teeth?" Adam complains, holding his mouth. "They hurt."

He's wearing the pair of wooden teeth Mr. Chips brought in today.

I mean the wooden teeth that *Mr. Wolcott* brought in today.

It turns out that Mr. Chips wasn't his real name.

"Yes! You are George Washington," says our new director. "Do you think our first president enjoyed wearing his teeth? Of course not! Imagine a two-by-four hammered into your gums. It's dreadful. As Shakespeare wrote, 'I pray thee, peace. I will be flesh and blood; for there was never yet philosopher that could endure the toothache patiently.'"

"Uh, okay," answers Adam, scratching his head.

Mr. Wolcott spurts a lot of nonsense, but he has made the play better already. Tomorrow's Friday, though. I'm not sure if he has enough time to fix everything.

I was surprised to see Mr. Chips—sorry, Mr. Wolcott—this morning. We were all surprised.

But it was a great idea for Samantha to bring him in. I guess she and Eric cooked up the plan.

It's just too bad they didn't cook it up sooner.

Mr. Wolcott immediately took control this morning. Everyone was happy except Maggie. She seemed annoyed, at first. I heard her tell him, "This is *my* play! Who invited you?"

But then I saw her talking with Eric and Samantha, and she huddled with Lacey and Paige a few minutes later at Paige's desk. After that, she seemed fine. She actually looked relieved.

Mr. Wolcott is terrific, too. He shows the actors where to stand, how to talk, and even how to project their voices so the entire audience can hear them. He's on top of everything.

"More regal!" he yells to Lizzie as she walks across the room. "You waddle like a duck. Martha Washington is the First Lady. She doesn't waddle. Chin up! Shoulders back! No—more bounce!"

Who knew there were so many different ways to walk?

Yow. Yow. Yow.

Mr. Wolcott was a world-famous director, or so he says. He has directed hundreds of plays. Maybe thousands.

Maggie stands next to Mr. Wolcott, nodding her head and smiling.

I can't remember the last time I saw her smile. Maybe never.

She should smile more. It looks good on her. Her gleaming white teeth are so straight, too.

I think:

With her smile, that nose, and soft eyes to boot—
Who knew a brain like her could be so cute?

"Thrust your arm when you speak," Mr. Wolcott tells Madelyn. "You're John Adams! A leader among men! But your hand movements are like that of a girl."

"But I *am* a girl," says Madelyn.

"But your part is not. In the theater you are what you perform. You are playing the part of the great John Adams, our second president. Be him! Feel him! Thrust your arm bravely and with purpose. More thrust! More!"

Madelyn thrusts her left arm forward and accidentally punches Adam in the arm. "Sorry."

"A little less thrust, perhaps," says Mr. Wolcott.

Our new director wheeled in a giant trunk this morning. It was crammed with costumes. He gave Adam a George Washington wig, a Revolutionary army coat, and that old set of wooden teeth.

The teeth are old, cracked, and sized for an adult. They look horribly uncomfortable. But they get the point across.

Wooden teeth play a big role in our musical.

Cooper was given a black overcoat, a frilly white shirt, and a white wig. He's like a shorter, plumper Thomas Jefferson. Somehow he's already gotten chocolate stains on his shirt, though.

Emmy has a red, white, and blue apron and a simple white bonnet that practically screams, *I'm Betsy Ross!*

Mr. Wolcott brought costumes for the villagers and the rest of the cast, too.

Yow. Yow. Yow.

He also gave our set decorators ideas—Giovanna and Samantha are painting a giant American flag on an old sheet. A fan will blow on it from the back of the stage so that it waves during the final scene.

Oh, say does that star-spangled banner yet wave
O'er the land of the free and the home of the brave?

That's not one of my rhymes, but it's pretty good.

Mr. Wolcott has put Danny and Jasmine in charge of fireworks. He said he wanted a "Grand display!" I'm a little nervous about that. But he can't mean real fireworks, right?

"A great actor talks from the diaphragm," Mr. Wolcott tells the cast. "The diaphragm is just below your chest. Speak from your gut. Project your voice. Emote—and stardom shall be yours. Remember: 'The play's the thing!' Or so says Hamlet."

"Sure. Whatever," says Adam, looking puzzled.

I notice someone standing behind me. It's Eric, and I wonder how long he's been there. "Yeah?" I ask.

"I've been working on your play. It's good, but I have just a few suggestions." Eric holds up a thick pile of papers. He puts them on my desk. It's my script, filled with red marks and scribbled words and extra scenes stuffed inside on loose paper. Eric looks down and mumbles, "I hope you don't mind."

He has just *a few* suggestions? It looks like he rewrote the entire thing.

I feel like hurling an eraser at him.

But then I hear Brian and Seth laugh. They're horsing around in the back.

They're not laughing at me, or even talking to me lately. They're still mad because I refuse to throw erasers anymore, and because I'm being responsible and stuff.

I look back at Soda's empty cage and gulp. She's still missing, and I've looked everywhere. That's the sort of thing that happens when you're good for nothing. You lose things, like hamsters and baby brothers.

I turn back to Eric and put down the eraser in my hand.

"Let me see what you have," I say, flipping over the first page.

"I really liked your songs," Eric says, "but I thought a few things needed to be more accurate."

I continue thumbing through his comments.

I have to admit that some of his ideas make sense.

A lot of them make sense.

Okay, all of them make sense.

For instance, Eric doesn't know where we would get all the fake blood and limbs for the big Battles of Lexington and Concord reenactment.

I guess he's right.

That scene where the colonists win the Battle of Gettysburg with their army of stormtrooper clones?

Eric crossed out the entire thing.

"Grab a seat and let's get to work," I tell him. Eric smiles and sits next to me.

We work through the script, line by line. Every change gets me excited. We are making it better, although losing the superpowered Ben Franklin scenes are hard.

I insist we keep the George Washington wooden teeth stuff, though.

I'm sure his wooden teeth played a big role in the American Revolution.

Well, I'm pretty sure.

Every few minutes someone interrupts us with his or her own ideas. Lizzie insists we need more romance between George and Martha Washington.

"People love romance," she claims. "That's why movies always have lots of kissing."

"Not the movies I watch," I say.

"The ones I watch do," Lizzie says, staring at Adam and sighing.

We add in some mushy stuff.

"I want to do an interpretive dance," says Ryan, spinning over to us.

"Why?" I ask.

"Because I like to dance and everyone loves dancing. In fact, I think I should do two dances, don't you?"

So we tell her to make up some dances. She smiles and spins away.

Eric and I are still revising when I notice the class has grown quiet. I assume that means something is dreadfully wrong.

I mean, it's been hours since something has gone dreadfully wrong.

I think of Soda, and I hope the class silence doesn't mean someone found her and she's hurt. I'd never forgive myself.

But I'm mistaken. This is not something that has gone dreadfully wrong, but something that has gone dreadfully *right*. Lizzie stands in front of the room. She holds a cardboard box filled with cupcakes. They have white frosting with red and blue stripes, like little American flags.

"I made these last night to celebrate our play," she says.

Yow. Yow. Yow.

I was dreadfully wrong about something going dreadfully wrong.

Because nothing can go wrong when cupcakes are involved.

I jump out of my seat and join the rest of the class swarming around Lizzie's box. I grab the biggest cupcake I see.

"What's in them?" I ask Lizzie right before burying my teeth into the moist yellow cake.

"It's sort of a secret, but I think I can trust you guys," says Lizzie. "I mean, we've all kept a much bigger secret, right? Anyway, it's made with ground tuna. Fudge. Cottage cheese. It's my own recipe. I call it tuna cupcake surprise!"

Imagine eating old gym shoes wrapped inside a dirty sponge and filled with bologna.

These taste worse.

My taste buds scream in agony. I nudge Lacey out of the way as I dash to the trash can. I spit the cupcake out and keep spitting until every last crumb is gone. But my mouth continues to suffer from the aftertaste, which is even worse than the before taste.

Pretty much everyone in class is gathering around the trash can, spitting cake out of their mouths, too.

Those who have not yet taken a bite of a cupcake look thankful, tossing away their dessert without trying it.

They are the lucky ones.

"These are awesome," says Adam as he chews his cupcake. He actually swallows it. He has a smile on his face, but sweat drips down his forehead and he looks slightly sick. "Can I have another one?" he asks bravely, with a gulp.

"Of course," says Lizzie, staring at Adam with a big smile as she chews one of those horrible desserts, too. I'm not sure if she even notices the rest of us holding our throats and gagging.

Adam grabs another cupcake. He takes a bite and smiles, but his hands tremble.

"With my cold, I can't even taste them," says Jade, chewing her cake and sniffling. "But I'm sure they're great."

I run past them, joining the rest of the class dashing out of the room and toward the drinking fountain.

Fortunately, no teacher sees us running in the halls, holding our throats.

35
MAGGIE

What a day at school. It feels like a hundred-ton weight has been lifted from my shoulders. Even Mom notices. "You're feeling better?" she asks at the dinner table as I scoop myself a second helping of au gratin potatoes.

"I feel excellent. Superb. Exquisite," I tell her. We don't talk about last night.

That's one thing about my parents—they give me my space. Dad sometimes says, "Great leaders need to be left alone to lead."

I've always agreed with him, but I'm not so sure anymore. I think leaders sometimes need help, too.

Before class began, Paige and Lacey walked up to me, just like they have every morning. But rather than being left alone to lead, like Dad says, and before they could even ask me the question I knew they were going to ask for the forty-seventh time, I handed them a manila folder. "Can you guys create a few work sheets for science?" I asked. "All the information you need is right here. It would be a big help."

Lacey and Paige looked stunned, but then a smile spread over Paige's face that could have lit a city block. Lacey had the same expression, too. "We'd love to! Thanks!"

"I knew I could count on you guys," I said.

But that wasn't the only thing that made me feel great today.

Mr. Wolcott came in like a white horse, riding in with the cavalry. I admit I was annoyed at first.

But Paige and Lacey needed assistance creating their work sheets, and I couldn't do that *and* direct at the exact same time, even if I wanted to. So I tore myself away from Mr. Wolcott, and when I looked back . . . he was making the play better. A lot better.

A giant, humongous, and gargantuan lot better.

We've still got a long way to go to get this play performance-ready. But a few rays of sunlight are peeking through the gray clouds.

I can't remember the last time anything looked so bright.

Even the work sheets that Lacey and Paige created were good. Really good.

At the table, I put down my napkin after my final bite of potatoes. We're done with dinner and I ask Mom, "Do you need help clearing the dishes?"

She nods gratefully. "Thanks, honey."

"I know how nice it is to get some help sometimes," I say.

I grab Dad's plate. He's still upset that I've dismissed Harvard as my future, but we haven't talked about it. I suppose there's a chance I could still get in. I guess I don't need to decide that *today*.

Right now, I just want to think about all the things that are going right. Because maybe, possibly, we're actually going to pull this off.

36
ADAM

When my ma wakes me up for school, I can barely move. I feel like I haven't slept in a week.

"Rise and shine, love," she says.

I moan and open my eyes. I squint. The only light is from the hallway outside, but it feels brighter than a flashlight shining in my pupils.

When I sit up, I shiver. Every part of me feels like it's submerged in ice. I want to bury myself back inside my blankets.

I roll my legs out of bed and my belly twitches. My mouth fills with spit, and it tastes like old eggs and tuna.

My stomach hurts, too.

"I think I'm going to throw up," I warn.

And then I do, right on the floor.

I put weight on my legs, avoiding the puddle of green and yellow by my feet, and stagger to the bathroom. I need to get dressed. Tonight is our big school play. We have to rehearse. I need to learn my new lines.

Kyle and Eric made a ton of changes yesterday. They've made the play a lot better, but it's hard to remember what lines have been taken away, and what lines are new.

I can't be late to school today. I'm George Washington. I'm the star.

For once, I'm actually glad I pulled the short straw. I think our play will be a big success. And with Lizzie playing Martha Washington, I couldn't be luckier.

"Where do you think you're going?" Ma asks.

"School," I say, but it feels like someone else is talking. My voice sounds distant, as if it's coming from another room.

"Back to bed, young man," my ma orders.

I take a step forward, but the room spins. I nod, return to my bed, and gratefully crawl back under the covers. The school needs me, but my bed needs me more.

"You might have the stomach flu," my ma warns.

"Or maybe it's food poisoning," I say with a forced smile. "From the homework, detention slip pad, and sneakers I ate in school."

"What?" asks Ma.

"Never mind," I mumble, trying to ignore the lingering tuna taste in my mouth.

I'm almost positive I have food poisoning, and I'm also almost positive it was Lizzie's cupcakes that made me sick.

I wonder if anyone else feels the same way I do.

37
ERIC

I wipe peanut butter from my hand onto a tissue from the teacher's desk. Kyle researched hamsters and learned they like peanut butter, so I helped him hide some peanut butter crackers behind the trash can. Hopefully, they'll lure Soda out from wherever she's been hiding. Today is our last day of school before winter break. I hate to think of Soda out of her cage for two more weeks.

The cleaning crew will feed her while we're gone, just like they do over the weekends. I remember Ms. Bryce telling us that. But they won't feed her if she's not in her cage.

I just hope nothing horrible happened to the poor girl. She probably feels alone. I know the feeling. But feeling alone doesn't have anything to do with *being* alone. You can feel alone anywhere, even in a classroom with twenty other kids.

I suppose I've always felt a little like Soda, but I don't feel that way now.

Kyle clapped my back this morning, and he didn't do it to hurt me, but just to say hello. Lacey smiled at me. She's never even noticed me before. For the first time in a long time, it doesn't feel so frightening here.

Kyle and I made a lot of revisions to the script. Everyone agrees the play is much improved. Maggie personally thanked me for helping.

It was kind of nice to feel part of the group.

The play still isn't completely accurate, though. A couple of scenes aren't in the correct order of events. A few things didn't happen exactly like we say they did, either. We all know that. But it's more accurate than it was, and some of the most ridiculous parts have been removed. I walk to Kyle, holding a few more small script notes in my hands. I'm proud of my changes. I can't wait to share them.

I smile, just a little. I don't think I've ever been excited to share anything in class before.

I look around the room. Adam hasn't shown up yet, and neither has Jade. Jade just has a small role in the play tonight. She's one of the townspeople. But Adam is the lead. George Washington! He better show up soon. He needs the rehearsal time.

Mr. Wolcott has made a difference as big as our script changes. Maybe even a bigger difference. He claims he is a famous director, and I believe him. He says a lot of things, and I'm not always sure what's the truth and what he's making up.

We all applauded when he walked in this morning. His face turned red and he mumbled, "Oh, much ado about nothing," before ordering the actors to their places.

And Samantha and Giovanna's sets are looking better. Some other kids help them finish the last couple of backdrops. Even Seth is assisting—he's painting a sign for Ryan. But Brian refuses to do anything except throw erasers at people.

Brian's out of the room on lookout duty right now, so he's not bothering anyone. Good.

The phone rings and Maggie reaches for the receiver. The actors stop acting and Mr. Wolcott stops directing. The class grows quiet. Things have been going so well. Maybe it's nothing.

But the classroom phone ringing is never a good sign.

Maggie, phone in her ear, keeps nodding and says, "Uh-huh," and "Oh my." She frowns, and her lips quiver. Her eyes bulge. When she finally hangs up the phone, she's pulling her hair. "We have bad news," she says, her voice cracking. "That was Mrs. Frank. Adam is home sick with the stomach flu or food poisoning or something. So is Jade. They're not coming to school. We're doomed."

Maggie pales, with a slight hint of green.

Lizzie's face is kind of green, too. She's standing behind Maggie, clutching her stomach and bending over.

"We can't perform the play without our star!" wails Maggie.

"I don't feel good," mumbles Lizzie.

"Adam is sick!" complains Maggie.

"I think I'm going to be sick, too," complains Lizzie, who then rushes toward the door and bolts straight out of the room.

"She'll be fine," says Maggie as the door closes behind Lizzie. "She better be," she adds with a gulp. "Or even our doom is doomed."

Doomed. Maggie is right. We're performing *tonight*! Without a George Washington, we have no play. And Lizzie is Martha Washington. Our secret has to leak, for sure. And we were so close to succeeding, too. Our play was good! Kyle looks at me, and his frown matches mine.

"Everything has gone wrong ever since Ms. Bryce left," complains Lacey.

"We wouldn't be having any of these problems if we had a real teacher," says Emmy. Then, to Mr. Wolcott, she adds, "No offense."

"None taken," says Mr. Wolcott. "The fool doth think himself to be wise, but the wise man knows himself to be a fool."

We all nod our heads as if we have some idea what he's talking about, although we don't.

After a brief pause, Jasmine says glumly, "I sort of wish we had a teacher."

"Me too," says Madelyn, also glumly.

"I miss Ms. Bryce's smiley faces," says Giovanna. "She used to draw the best smiley faces on my homework."

"Remember when she brought in candy bars for everyone on Halloween?" asks Cooper. "That was nice."

"She complimented my hair once," Samantha says, with a sad, faraway look.

"About a month ago, my mom and I saw her at the mall," says Danny. "And she said the nicest things about me even though I stepped on her foot and ruined one of her shoes."

"And we have more homework now than we did then," complains Eli. The entire class groans, and then looks at Maggie.

"All that homework isn't my fault," says Maggie. As we stare at her, Maggie glares back, and then looks away with a sigh. "Well, maybe it's my fault just a little." She coughs. "It seemed like a good idea." Her shoulders slump. She has looked exhausted all week, but suddenly she stands up taller. It's as if a huge weight has just rolled off her back. "I think we should tell the truth and get a real teacher."

"But what if they give us Drill Sergeant DeWitt again?" Emmy asks.

"I guess we'll have to take the chance," says Paige. "Besides, my sister had her as a sub for her fourth-grade class, and she heard that Sergeant DeWitt is being shipped over-seas to join her platoon."

"Really?" asks Cooper. The corners of his eyes crinkle from his relieved smile. He's holding a candy bar, and he takes a large bite out of it.

I nod my head, too. We've done pretty well without a teacher, but the thought of having one feels reassuring. Maybe it *is* time to tell the truth.

In fact, revealing our simply unbelievable secret doesn't feel so scary anymore. It feels comforting.

Mom is going to go crazy when she finds out. But I'll get through it. Besides, I have friends in class now. You can get through anything if you have friends.

The entire class seems relieved at the thought of sharing our secret. It's like a collective deep breath flows through the class, as if someone has punctured a big balloon that's been getting ready to pop, getting ready to pop, getting ready to pop, and then BOOM! The pressure is gone and the air feels calmer.

I guess too much freedom stops being fun after a while. Everyone needs some rules, every now and then.

I wonder if that's how the American settlers felt after the Revolutionary War. The British had all these rules, and the colonists hated them for it. So they fought for their freedom. But when they won the war, did they run around without any rules at all? No, they made new rules. And appointed their own leader.

"Anyone who talks is a sock hater and smells like a sock, or whatever!" shouts Brian, breaking the silence, his mouth sneering. I thought he was still on lookout duty, but I guess I was wrong.

Everyone in class glares at him, and Brian seems to deflate. He shrugs. "Fine. No one is a sock hater or smeller, okay?" He looks at his backpack and sighs. "I can't believe I've been carrying that stupid sock in my backpack for two years, too." He winds his arm back and then whips his eraser at Seth. Seth ducks, but the rubbery projectile bounces off his back. "One point!" he yells. The rest of the class ignores him.

"Let's call Principal Klein," says Maggie, picking up the phone on the teacher's desk, "and ask for a teacher."

"Do you think they'll let us perform the play?" asks Cooper. "I really wanted to be onstage."

"Probably not," says Maggie.

Murmurs spread through the class. No one likes the idea of wasting all our hard work.

"I really like my Paul Revere costume," adds Trevor, running his fingers along his brown vest.

"I've memorized all my lines, and it was hard," says Cooper.

"My part was hard to memorize, too," says Gavin, although he only has his one line.

"And it would be a shame not to use our sets," says Giovanna, glancing at the large paper backdrops taped against the far wall. One depicts a farm scene, one backdrop shows a city street back in 1776, and one is of the interior of Carpenters' Hall, which is where the First Continental Congress met. There is also the giant American flag.

Most need a few finishing touches to complete, but they look impressive.

"One more day keeping our secret can't hurt, right?" asks Paige.

"The show must go on!" declares Mr. Wolcott.

Maggie puts down the phone receiver without making a call. "Then it's settled. We'll keep our secret until after the play," she says. "And then we'll tell the truth."

So that's that. The play will be performed and our script will be shared. Then, after the show, we'll spill our incredible secret.

Kyle and I exchange huge grins.

"But we still have a problem," Maggie adds. "We don't have anyone to play George Washington, remember? It's the biggest part, too. No one will be able to memorize it in time."

Right. Adam's sick. In my excitement I had completely forgotten.

"I can play the role," says Mr. Wolcott. "Did I mention my life onstage with the famed Franny Bree? We were truly marvelous together."

"That's nice of you to offer," says Maggie. "But I really think a kid needs to play the part."

I slink in my seat. If I dropped a staple, the class would hear it. That's how quiet we are. No one volunteers. No one can memorize the part in time, anyway.

I peek at Kyle. He's holding an eraser, and from the angry glare on his face and the way he wiggles the pink rubber in his hands, I think he wants to chuck it at someone. He frowns with a look of such disappointment that I feel sorry for the Big Goof. Although really, now that I know him better, Kyle's not much of a goof at all.

If only someone had Adam's part memorized.

But someone does.

I clear my throat. I unslink. I grab my desk so hard my knuckles turn white. "Wait a second," I say. I gulp. I want to disappear, but instead I say, "I helped write the part, right? So I know it. I can do it."

I want to capture those words and stick them back in my mouth. But it's too late now. You can't swallow words after they blurt out.

Once words are out in the world, they are out there forever, whether you speak them, text them, or declare your freedom from the British government.

Maggie smiles. Jasmine claps me on the back. Kyle shouts, "All right, Eric!" I walk to the front of the class, and everyone cheers.

My legs shake. I regret volunteering, despite the ovation.

"Well done," says Mr. Wolcott as I join him and the rest of the actors. "How far that little candle throws his beams."

Part of me wants to run away screaming, but a bigger part of me wants to stay right where I am. I'm excited and petrified at the same time.

"What's wrong?" asks Maggie. She must notice the look of fright and doubt that is probably spread across my face.

I bite my lip. "It's just that I don't like speaking up in front of people," I admit. I feel embarrassed saying it.

"What are you talking about?" she says, as if shocked by my answer. "You always speak up."

I shake my head. Maybe she has me confused with Brian or Kyle, although we look nothing alike. They're twice as big as me. No, they are three times as big as me.

"Of course you do," Maggie insists. "How many times have you saved us when a teacher has asked where Ms. Bryce is? Who suggested we share lunches on our very first day after Ms. Bryce quit? Who suggested we assign a lookout? Whose writing has helped save our play?"

I said all that? I did all that?

"And it was your idea to ask Mr. Wolcott to direct the play, not mine," adds Samantha, who I didn't notice behind me.

I blink. I look at Samantha, and then at Maggie. I've shared a lot with the class, even though I didn't think I did.

I think about how I've always felt like a quiet, dull plant. But maybe it's better to be a blooming, colorful flower, even at the risk of getting plucked. Maybe that's sort of the point of being a flower.

"Ready to rehearse?" asks Mr. Wolcott.

I nod. "Yeah. But one more thing first." I look at Maggie and take a deep breath. "I think we need to write a letter. All of us. Together."

Maggie nods. "Actually, I think we need to write *two* letters."

The door opens. My heart skips a beat, fearing it's Principal Klein. Our secret will be leaked hours before we planned.

But it is just Lizzie. "I'm better now," she says, her hand covering her mouth. And then she puffs out her cheeks. "No, I'm not!" She runs back out the door and into the hallway.

38
MAGGIE

I knew we were performing a play in front of *people*. Obviously. We didn't write, rehearse, build props, and prepare amid a million panic attacks to perform in front of a crowd of mice. But *still*. There is a huge, vast, cavernous difference between *thinking* of a crowd and actually seeing one waiting for you.

I peek through the curtains. The auditorium is full. Standing room only.

I'm not *in* the play, thankfully. There would be absolutely no way I could perform in front of this many people.

Eric looks petrified. But he volunteered for it!

"Quite a turnout," says Lacey, smiling. I nod. My knees shake just looking at the throngs of parents and people waiting for our performance. Every fifth-grade parent in the school must be here, plus brothers, sisters, grandparents, aunts, uncles, and who knows who else.

They are here to see our play, which starts in six minutes.

Gulp.

"This is so exciting," says Lacey, standing beside me. "Oh, and Paige and I created a couple of new work sheets. I know we don't have to, with winter break starting and everything else, but we wanted to try. It was fun, but hard. I don't know how you did it all by yourself."

I nod, grateful for her comment. "It wasn't as easy as I thought it would be," I admit.

"I'm glad I'm a kid and not a teacher," says Lacey.

I nod. "Yeah. Me too."

I continue to stare through the curtain. So many people are here just to see my play. To watch my directing!

But to be honest, even though the programs (Jasmine designed them and they are lovely) list me as the director, that's not totally correct. Mr. Wolcott deserves the credit. His direction saved the day. But he refused to be listed in the program. He said, "Reputation is an idle and most false imposition; oft got without merit, and lost without deserving."

As usual, I had no idea what he meant.

In the end, my contributions mostly consisted of getting out of the way and allowing Mr. Wolcott to take charge.

I have to admit that I've learned a lot from this entire experience. Funny, isn't it? I planned to do the teaching, and here I am doing the learning. I think I might have learned more from *not* having a teacher than I did *having* one.

I'm not talking about learning math and reading and academics, obviously. But I've learned how to be a better leader, for sure. I learned that being a great leader means trusting others. People can surprise you when you let them do stuff, like Kyle writing a play and Samantha finding Mr. Wolcott to help us and quiet Eric finding his voice.

Those are lessons that are far more important to learn than math.

Well, maybe not *far* more important. Math is vital to a solid education. But I'm already a whiz at math.

As I stand in the theater wing scanning the audience, I pat my pocket, which has one of the letters our class wrote. We'll share it after the play is performed.

I mailed the other letter, right after school ended, as planned. It should arrive at its address tomorrow.

Behind me, the actors get ready. Giovanna and Samantha push the final props into place. Mr. Wolcott takes the entire cast through some vocal warm-ups.

"I thought a thought, but the thought I thought was not the thought I thought I thought," the group chants together. These exercises are supposed to loosen lips and help actors speak better onstage.

"The free thugs set three thugs free! Say it!" commands Mr. Wolcott. "Enunciate! Tonight is the time for you to shine. Remember, be not afraid of greatness: some are born great, some achieve greatness, and some have greatness thrust upon them!"

"That's what I always say," says Cooper. We all look at him, perplexed. He shrugs. "I mean, you know, that's what I would say if I had any idea what it meant."

I inhale deeply, soaking in the excitement of being backstage, the buzz from the crowd, and the smell of vomit wafting through.

Barf. Upchuck. Ralph.

Wait—the smell of what?

That's when I hear the unmistakable and entirely disagreeable sound of someone getting sick. I think it must be nerves. It's an extremely unpleasant reaction to the excitement of performing, but not an entirely uncommon one. Many actors and athletes get sick before big performances or games, or so I've read.

It's Lizzie who is sick, but she doesn't look sick with nerves. She just looks sick. She's been groaning all day, but I assumed it would pass. She kept insisting she was fine, even while she ran to and from the bathroom. But she is not fine, not at all.

Lizzie is clutching her stomach and leaning over. Mr. Wolcott presses his hand against her forehead, and when he looks up, he appears as ill as Lizzie. "She's as sick as a dog! The show must go on, but our Martha Washington cannot."

But she has the second-biggest part in the entire musical. We need her. First Adam and Jade can't perform, and now Lizzie? We're dropping like swatted flies. Meanwhile, the crowd beyond the curtain waits for us. We're supposed to perform in four and a half minutes! We're doomed.

I look at Mr. Wolcott. He was a famous theater director. This sort of thing probably happens all the time. He must have some ready-made solution, some tried-and-true formula all great theater directors rely on to save the day when actors get sick.

A plan. A scheme. A stratagem.

"What do we do?" asks Kyle.

Mr. Wolcott scratches his head. He doesn't *look* like he has a plan. But then he opens his mouth. He will recite a quote that none of us will understand but will turn gray clouds into blue skies. "Do we have an understudy? Someone else who has learned the part?"

"I don't think so," says Kyle.

Mr. Wolcott coughs. "Then I have no idea. Sorry."

I scream. I can't help it. I stand there and let loose a high, earsplitting yowl.

My doom is complete.

When I finish my wail of anguish, everyone looks at me. My legs quiver. I feel like everyone is waiting for me to solve our problem. I should do *something*. I'm the class leader.

I take a deep breath. I open my mouth. I remember what I've learned about teamwork and asking for help. Trevor stands next to me, and I think he's about to roll his eyes, regardless of what I say. He'll probably say I'm bossy. I look at him. "What do you think we should do, Trevor?" I ask.

He steps back. I guess he wasn't expecting me to say *that*.

"Me?" he asks. I nod and hope that maybe he *does* have a solution. Trevor shrugs. "How should I know? You're the one in charge."

I look around to the rest of my classmates. I realize that if we fail, I could still go to Harvard. Of course I could. I've got a whole lot of years left to impress them, and I'm only a kid right now. But still, I wanted our class to shine tonight. We all worked so hard.

"Can't we just skip her parts?" asks Jasmine.

"I don't see how," says Kyle. "She's in a lot of scenes."

"And I won't know when to say my lines," complains Cooper.

"Me either," says Gavin, although he only has his one line and he still can't remember it, anyway.

We've all formed a circle, a circle of doom I suppose, when Samantha steps into the middle. She clears her throat. Her daddy can't buy us out of this one, although I wish he could.

"I'll do it," she says. "I know the part. I've read the script about a million times, and I have the entire thing memorized. Even the new parts."

She does? She will? My mouth is open in shock, and when I scan the rest of us in our circle, all of *their* mouths are open in shock, too. Samantha is the last person I would have expected to volunteer. I guess I'm still learning lessons about trusting people.

I used to think all of my classmates were blockheads. But that's not true at all. If anything, *I'm* the blockhead for thinking that.

"Then let's get you dressed," declares Mr. Wolcott. "Now is the winter of our discontent made glorious summer by this son of York."

"Sure, I guess," I say, confused.

"Can we skip the romantic parts?" Samantha asks Eric.

Eric looks relieved. "Yes! Please!"

I remove the wig from Lizzie's head and lower it onto Samantha's while Mr. Wolcott ties the Martha Washington frock around her waist.

"Good luck," I tell her.

"Never good luck," Mr. Wolcott declares. "In the theater we say, 'Break a leg.'"

"I don't want her to break her leg!" I insist.

"It's meant to be ironic," says Eric.

"Fine. Break a leg," I say with a shrug as the curtains part and the actors hurry to their places.

39
ERIC

LET LIBERTY FALL!
WRITTEN BY KYLE ANDERSON AND ERIC HILL

(ACT 1, SCENE 1: THE ORIGIN OF
THE AMERICAN FLAG)

Right before the curtains part, I adjust my white wig and run to my place onstage, next to the fake tree stump. I'm supposed to be a teenager in this scene, so instead of wearing my blue army coat I'm wearing a blue hoodie. I pretend to sob, and there's an ax on the ground next to me.

The crowd claps and I hear my mom yell, "That's my Eric!" I think I'm blushing, but I doubt anyone can see from the audience.

Samantha, playing the future Martha Washington, is dressed in a simple frock and bonnet. She crosses the stage. "Teenage Georgie Washington—why are you so upset?"

I hold my jaw. I'm wearing Mr. Wolcott's pair of fake wooden teeth in my mouth, and they are at least two sizes too big for me. I have to open my mouth really wide to talk. "Hello, future Martha Washington. I cannot tell a lie. I cut down this cherry tree. And now my father has grounded me."

"You're spitting on me," she says.

"Sorry. It's the teeth."

She takes a step backward, so she's out of spray range. "If you're the father of our country, is your father the grandfather of our country?"

"I cannot tell a lie. Yes." When I talk, a little more spit flies out and hits the bottom of her frock. "Sorry."

She frowns and takes another step back. "But why did you cut down the tree, teenage Georgie Washington?"

I hold my jaw. My gums ache. "I wanted to build a new set of wooden teeth because woodpeckers ate my old pair."

"Woodpeckers are interesting unless you have a wooden leg or wooden teeth or you're a wooden puppet like Pinocchio. Then woodpeckers can be scary."

I nod. According to the script, we're supposed to hug each other and kiss. Lizzie insisted on adding that part. I squirm a little.

"We're skipping over the romantic parts, right?" Samantha asks, keeping her distance.

"I cannot tell a lie. Yes," I answer, relieved.

"I have a dream," says Samantha. "That someday I'll be first lady, you'll be president, and we'll have our own country, which we'll call the United States of America." As she talks, she walks across the stage and back.

"Nice walk," I whisper. "Very regal."

"Thank you."

I stand up and place my hand on my heart. "Future Martha Washington, although I'm only the teenage George Washington, you have convinced me. I vow that when I grow up, I will fight for our independence and for better wooden teeth. Especially wooden teeth."

"Oh, teenage Georgie Washington! I hope so," says Samantha. "A land built on wooden teeth would be a wonderful place." She pauses. "We're supposed to kiss again, but we can ignore that, right?"

"I'll sign my name big!" yells Gavin, rushing onto the stage.

"Get out of here," I whisper to him, waving him away. "Your part isn't until the second half. And you're not even saying it right."

"Sorry," says Gavin, rushing off the stage.

A couple of people in the audience laugh. Maybe they think that was in the script. As we follow Gavin offstage, the audience breaks into applause.

They really liked the first scene. Samantha and I high-five just offstage.

"You're a really good actor," she says to me.

"You too," I answer truthfully. "Just as good as Lizzie. Maybe better."

(ACT 1, SCENE 3: THE BOSTON TEA
PARTY IS PLANNED)

I watch from backstage as the curtains rise on colonial Boston. The backdrop shows narrow cobblestone streets winding between small brick buildings. Samantha and Giovanna did a great job creating it. To make sure the audience knows this is Boston, Giovanna wrote "This is Boston" at the top of the backdrop.

Cooper, who plays Thomas Jefferson, hurries across the stage. He wears a thick woolen coat on this crisp autumn evening. Coyotes howl through the cold, echoing streets.

"There are supposed to be howling winds, not howling coyotes," I whisper to Danny. He's standing next to me.

"That is my howling wind," Danny insists, frowning. "I'm doing my best."

Ryan, playing a villager, spins onto the stage. She wears a black, three-sided colonial hat, a frilly white shirt, and waves a picket sign that says NO T TAX!

"Down with the British! Boo!" Ryan yells. She stops spinning.

Seth is next to me in the wings, too, watching. He painted Ryan's sign. "It must have been really hard back then," he whispers to me. "Every time you said the letter *T*, you were taxed."

"Actually, they taxed the drinking tea," I say.

Seth looks away, nodding. "That makes more sense."

Back onstage, Ryan and Cooper are talking about taxation and stuff.

"Don't worry. I have a plan," says Cooper. "If it's all right, I'll sing it to you."

"Of course," says Ryan. "And I will perform an original interpretive dance. With spinning."

As Cooper sings his solo, Ryan performs an interpretive dance, with a lot of spinning. The song is sung to the tune of "You're a Grand Old Flag."

It's a taxed tea bag.
It's a high-priced tea bag.
It's a tax we simply can't afford.
We'll all scream and shout.
We'll toss the tea out—
Into the harbor, overboard.

It's an uprising
Over Darjeeling.
The king's an ignorant burping moose.
We'll give history

Quite a tea party!
And we'll only drink apple juice.

The audience claps along to the song. Kyle stands on the opposite side of the wing. I don't think he could smile any wider.

Onstage, other villagers have joined Ryan and Cooper, singing together. They all wear distinctive colonial clothes such as waistcoats, breeches, and stockings. Near the back of the stage, Ryan continues to spin.

It's just not okay
To tax our Earl Grey.
Why, we have clearly been betrayed.
With our taxes up,
We'll all skip a cup—
And instead drink pink lemonade.

Jasmine adds, *"And fruit punch!"*

The other villagers stare at her. That wasn't in the script. She shrugs. "Hey, I don't like lemonade, okay?"

The villagers raise their fists and march off the stage shouting, "Down with the British!" and "No taxation without representation!"

Ryan, who must be dizzy from all of that spinning, trips, and then stumbles after them.

"Ta-da!" she says right before leaving the stage.

The audience cheers. I look over to Kyle. I was wrong about his smile not being able to get any wider. Because I think it's a lot bigger now.

(ACT 1, SCENE 6: CREATION OF THE FIRST CONTINENTAL CONGRESS)

The curtain opens to reveal a small meeting room. Emmy, who plays Betsy Ross, wears a red, white, and blue dress and holds an American flag. I face her, along with Cooper and Madelyn, who plays the part of John Adams. We all wear big white wigs.

The wig itches, but it's not nearly as annoying as these wooden teeth.

"What do you think?" Emmy asks. "I sewed this flag all by myself. See? It has fifty stars, one for each state."

"But there are only thirteen colonies," says Cooper. "How do you know we'll have fifty states someday?"

"Just a lucky guess."

Next to me, Cooper and Madelyn, or rather Thomas Jefferson and John Adams, admire the flag, murmuring their approval and patting Emmy on the back. "Well done, Betsy . . . Very stripy . . . Why five-pointed stars?"

"We need more than a flag," I announce, stepping forward. "We need laws, congress, and most of all, a new set of wooden teeth. And a bunch of other stuff, like a White House. Or my name isn't George Washington!"

"Let's elect a congress to put all of those things together," suggests Madelyn. She steps forward and throws out her arm, punching me in the shoulder. "Sorry. That was my manly arm thrust."

"I cannot tell a lie: That hurt," I say, wincing. "Although not as much as these wooden teeth do."

The audience giggles, although there is nothing funny about my teeth, at least not to me.

Madelyn steps forward, away from me, and thrusts out an arm again. She narrowly misses Emmy's head. "We will form the First Continental Congress, where we will discuss liberty and other things. Then, after we fight the British, we can elect George Washington our first president. Me, John Adams, will be our second president. Thomas Jefferson will be our third president."

"But I want to be the second president," complains Cooper.

"Too bad. I called it already," says Madelyn.

"This will be great!" exclaims Emmy as Betsy Ross. "I'll make Lizzie's special tuna cupcake surprise dessert for the meeting."

"How about apple pie instead?" Madelyn suggests. She thrusts out her arm and just misses clocking Emmy on the chin.

"Watch it," hisses Emmy.

Gavin rushes onstage. "I'll sign my name huge!"

"Not yet," I whisper to him. "And that's not even the right line."

"Sorry," says Gavin, rushing off the stage.

(ACT 1, SCENE 8: WASHINGTON AGREES
TO LEAD THE ARMY)

It is evening on the streets of Philadelphia, although the backdrop looks exactly like the streets of Boston except Giovanna crossed out the word *Boston* and wrote *Philadelphia* underneath it. I'm onstage along with Samantha, Cooper, and Eli. Eli wears bifocals and holds a kite because he plays Ben Franklin. We huddle together in a semicircle, facing the audience.

My mouth aches. A few of my wooden teeth have twisted, and I can't close my mouth all the way. One tooth falls off and lands on the floor. "These teeth are killing me," I groan.

"Forget your teeth, George Washington," says Cooper, stepping to the side to avoid my spit. "The Continental Congress needs someone to lead our army against the British."

"I will defeat them with my superpowered Kite of Electrical Might!" declares Eli as Ben Franklin, holding out his kite and flexing a bicep.

"We killed that scene, remember?" I whisper to him.

"But a superpowered Kite of Electrical Might was way cooler than anything else in this play," Eli whines, crossing his arms and turning his back to us, moping.

I worry that Eli is ruining the play, but a few people in the audience laugh as if everything has been planned.

"You're the only one who can lead us, George Washington," says Samantha. She's supposed to then say, "Kiss me now!" but thankfully she skips that line.

"I cannot tell a lie," I say. "My mouth hurts too much to help."

"We still have my super mighty kite," suggests Eli.

I frown at him, or at least I try to. It's hard to frown with these teeth in my mouth.

"But you have to lead the army, or Wilbur Smelly-Sock will lead it," complains Cooper, playing Thomas Jefferson. "Then we'll have to name our new capital Smelly-Sock, DC, and we'll be the laughingstock of the world."

"We just have to name it Washington, DC, George!" Samantha exclaims. "And if you win the war, you can buy a new pair of wooden teeth."

"Or we can go with my idea and defeat the British army in, like, five seconds," Eli says.

"Enough with the stupid kite already," says Samantha, shoving Eli.

"I will lead the army, in the name of better teeth everywhere!" I step in between Samantha and Eli, who are taking turns pushing each other.

Samantha raises her hand to me. "Great! High five!"

The script says we're supposed to kiss and declare our love for each other, but I gladly give her a high five instead.

"Hurrah! Hurrah!" cheers Cooper.

A few people in the audience also yell, "Hurrah! Hurrah!" They seem to really be enjoying the play.

Eli is supposed to cheer, too, but he just stares at his kite and grumbles to himself.

"Let's sing another song," says Cooper.

"It seems like a good time for one," I agree.

Ryan dashes onto the stage and begins another interpretive dance in the background with a lot of spinning.

We all sing to the tune "When Johnny Comes Marching Home."

So Georgie can wear wood teeth again—
Hurrah! Hurrah!
He'll lead our troops of fighting men.
Hurrah! Hurrah!
Our boys will cheer and march about,
They'll brush teeth to keep cavities out,
And we'll all have bright smiles when—
Georgie wears wooden teeth.

We'll raise the flag and beat our drums.
Hurrah! Hurrah!

We'll take great care of our gums.
Hurrah! Hurrah!
We'll battle back the king's menace,
And twice a year visit dentists.
And we'll all have bright smiles when—
Georgie wears wooden teeth.

The enemy we'll smash and crush!
Hurrah! Hurrah!
Our fists we'll raise, our teeth we'll brush!
Hurrah! Hurrah!
We'll show those Brits who's the boss.
We'll win freedom and then we'll floss,
And we'll all have bright smiles when—
Georgie wears wooden teeth.

We march offstage. The crowd cheers us loudly, and a few people whistle. My mom yells, "That's my son! George Washington! Isn't he wonderful?" which is a little embarrassing, but I can't help but grin, anyway.

Ryan dances off behind us. She looks really dizzy from spinning, and as we near the side of the stage, she smashes into Samantha.

"Ta-da!" she shouts.

Eli is behind her, swooping with his arms flapping.

"What are you doing?" I ask him.

"Flying off with my mighty electrical superpowered kite powers."

"You know we killed that scene!" Samantha yells at him.

Gavin dashes past him and onto the stage. "I'll sign my name large!" he shouts.

"Not yet!" I whisper loudly. "And you're still not saying it right!"

The crowd applauds as the curtains close. If they realize how badly we're messing up, their cheers don't show it.

(ACT 2, SCENE 1: PAUL REVERE GETS HIS INSTRUCTIONS)

The curtains part, revealing Trevor, who plays Paul Revere, hammering horseshoes on a bench. I adjust my teeth, but they are half in my mouth and half hanging on my lip.

Three more teeth crack off.

"George! Welcome!" says Trevor, waving. "Your teeth are falling out."

"I cannot tell a lie, Paul Revere. I know they are. But we don't have time right now to talk teeth. We need you to warn the people the British are coming. We will light one lantern if they come by land, and two if by sea."

"What if I see three lanterns?" he asks.

"Then they come by airplane."

"Why can't Ben Franklin warn everyone with his super-powered Kite of Electrical Might?"

"Because we deleted all of that from the script."

"Oh, right. I forgot." Trevor steps forward with a long and purposeful stride. He puts his hands on his hips and looks out to the crowd. "Then I will do it. I will ride to Lexington and warn the people, crying, 'The British are here! The British are here!'"

"Actually, you need to shout, 'The British are coming! The British are coming!'"

"I think my way makes more sense, but if you insist. We will fight for freedom! For America!"

"And for wooden teeth!" I declare as more wood splinters out of my mouth. "Especially for wooden teeth."

Trevor runs off yelling, "The British are here! The British are here!"

"No, they're coming! They're coming! And you have to wait for the lanterns!"

(ACT 2, SCENE 4: JEFFERSON WRITES THE DECLARATION OF INDEPENDENCE)

Cooper sits at a desk in his study, writing with a quill on a large piece of parchment paper. I stand next to him along with Eli (as Ben Franklin, of course) and Gavin. Gavin plays John Hancock.

"If you had a superpowered quill, you'd be done writing that by now," says Eli.

"Op e we a spr prr suff awee," I say, slobbering.

"What?" asks Eli.

I can barely talk with those oversized wooden teeth in my mouth. I remove them and my jaw already feels better. "I said, 'Stop it with the superpower stuff already.' We must demand our independence. Thomas Jefferson, we need you to write a declaration."

Cooper nods. "We'll call it, Leave Us Alone, You Ignorant Burping Moose."

"That's catchy," I say. "But we were thinking of calling it the Declaration of Independence."

"I like my title better," says Cooper. He frowns, lifts his quill, and writes a few words on the parchment paper. We gather around him to watch. "I'll start with, 'We the people.' "

"Let's save that for the Constitution," I say.

"Good idea," agrees Cooper.

"I'll write my name supersized!" Gavin shouts.

"It's not time for your line yet," I say, rolling my eyes. "And you're still saying it wrong."

"Sorry," says Gavin.

"The Declaration of Independence is an important document," Cooper interrupts. "I think we should sing a song about it."

"That's a great idea. It seems about time for another song," I agree.

Ryan runs out behind us and starts spinning.

"Why are you here?" I ask. "We only agreed to two dances."

"I like to spin," she says with a shrug. "And dancing always entertains."

"I'll write my name ginormous!" Gavin shouts, stepping forward.

"Not yet," I say. "And that's not right, either."

Cooper, Eli, and I take turns singing lines of the song. We sing to the tune of "The Battle Hymn of the Republic."

We declare independence from that dirty rotten king.
We'll poke him in the eyeball and put his arm into a sling.
We will smack him in the head with fourteen pounds of
    jelly beans.
Our freedom marches on!

The king's armpits are stinky and his nose is filled with warts.
His hair is extra greasy. His breath smells like rotten farts.
His toes are warped and ugly, and he doesn't have a heart.
Our freedom marches on!

Glory, glory hallelujah!
Kick the king out as our ruler.
Democracy is way cooler.
Our freedom marches on!

We'll send our plea for liberty across the Atlantic.
Each one of us will sign our names—

Everyone looks at Gavin. "What?" he asks.

"It's time for your line," I hiss.

Gavin shouts, *"I'll sign my name gigantic!"*

"Nicely done," I say.

Cooper continues singing.

Give us freedom or we'll sink you like the Titanic!
Our freedom marches on!

We gather around, shaking hands and exchanging back slaps. The crowd is going nuts, cheering and whistling. Someone yells, "Bravo!" It might be my mom.

Things are going pretty well. Maybe I should share more of what I write.

Of course, things aren't exactly going perfectly, either. Ryan, dizzy from spinning so much, smashes into Eli and they both crash to the ground.

"If only I had my superpowered kite," moans Eli, holding his head.

"Ta-da," mumbles Ryan.

The crowd cheers even louder, as if it's all part of the script.

(ACT 2, SCENE 7: WAR BREAKS OUT)

Samantha and I are onstage, alone. The audience is hushed. Mr. Wolcott managed to get my wooden teeth back into my mouth, although barely. I wish he hadn't. It feels like I have a jaw full of chipped marbles. A giant American flag waves in back of us, although the offstage fan is cranked up to high and the wind blows off Samantha's bonnet. Danny makes loud duck calls from behind the curtain.

"You're supposed to be making explosion war sounds," I whisper loudly to him.

"These are my explosion sounds," Danny whispers back. "I'm doing my best."

"The script says we kiss now," Samantha says softly to me. "We won't, right?" I nod. "Good." She clears her throat. To the audience, she says loudly, "Now all we need is a country to wave our flag in, and fifty states, and a national anthem and stuff. And then, maybe, someday, fifth graders will put on plays about us." She looks at me, but I'm gazing off and holding my jaw. "George Washington, did you hear anything I said?"

"I cannot tell a lie. No. My teeth hurt too much to listen." That line is in the script, but I don't have to do much acting to make it believable, unfortunately.

"Someday kids will have dentists," Samantha says.

"I hope so. That's what we're fighting for."

Cooper walks onto the stage, followed by Gavin, Eli, Madelyn, Emmy, and Trevor. "You are wrong, George Washington," says Cooper. "We're fighting because we believe that all men are created equal, that they are endowed by their Creator with certain unalienable Rights."

The rest of the cast streams onto the stage, forming a single line in back of Samantha and me and facing the audience.

Madelyn steps forward and thrusts out a fist, punching me in the arm. "Sorry."

"You really need to watch your manly thrusts," I say, wincing.

"I'll sign my name gigantic!" shouts Gavin. Everyone ignores him.

Behind me, the entire cast continues to recite from the Declaration of Independence, together: "that among these are Life, Liberty and the pursuit of Happiness.—That to secure these rights, Governments are instituted among Men, deriving their just powers from the consent of the governed,—That whenever any Form of Government becomes destructive of these ends, it is the Right of the People to alter or to abolish it, and to institute new Government, laying its foundation on such principles and organizing its powers in such form, as to them shall seem most likely to effect their Safety and Happiness."

"And we also fight for dentistry. Just a little," I say, removing my teeth and massaging my pained jaw.

Eli steps forward. "This is where I soar across the room with my superpowered Kite of Electrical Might, while fireworks light up the stage, followed by explosive fireballs and a red, white, and blue ring of fire!" he announces.

"Um, no, we killed all that, remember?" I say as Danny and Jasmine run across the stage with sparklers.

The crowd stands up, cheering, as the curtains close.

40
SAMANTHA

Eric and I, the two leads, bow. We're onstage, just a few steps in front of the rest of the class. The applause rains down on us like a thunderstorm, although it's a very happy and excited thunderstorm.

I soak it in. I can't stop smiling. Maybe I should become a professional actress. I bet Daddy could get me some roles.

Or maybe I can get them myself. I don't think I need Daddy to do *everything* for me.

I did this. *I* earned the applause.

I think that's why it feels even better than I think applause is supposed to feel.

And the audience isn't clapping just for me, but for all my classmates. We all bow.

When you bow after a ballet recital solo, you're all alone onstage with no one to share your smile with. But here, now, I'm sharing my smile with all my classmates. That makes it feel even better.

I peek behind me. Emmy throws me a great big smile. Madelyn gives me a thumbs-up.

My friends think I did great.

It's funny to think of them that way. *My friends.*

They were terrific tonight, too. We all were. As Kyle would say, "Yow, yow, yow!"

Mom and Daddy clap, too. I see them way in the back. I thought they were too busy to come tonight, but Daddy's business meeting must have been canceled, and Mom's tennis match must have been postponed. Or maybe, just maybe, they canceled their appointments and came here to see me.

That would be something.

Aunt Karen is here, too. Her grin is just as huge as my parents', and she's clapping just as hard as them, if not harder.

The claps die down as Principal Klein walks up the stairs and onto the wings of the stage. He's wearing a bow tie with his orange cardigan sweater, but he still seems sort of scary to me. Eric and I move back, joining the rest of our class to give our principal plenty of room. He strolls to the front.

An uneasy feeling settles in my stomach. Because I know what's going to happen now.

We all agreed. It's too late to change our minds. And while I know it's for the best, I'm still nervous about it. I want the applause to continue, and not turn to angry murmurs, like I think it might.

Principal Klein smiles at us, and then addresses the audience.

"That was simply wonderful, wasn't it?" he asks the crowd. He claps, and they respond with more cheers and whistles. We bow—the entire class together—one more time.

It feels nice to bow together.

One final bow, before the end.

Principal Klein turns to us. "Did your class write the play yourselves?"

"Kyle and Eric wrote it," says Ryan.

"Very impressive," says Principal Klein. "Kyle and Eric, why don't you step forward?"

They do, and the crowd erupts again. A short, plump woman—she must be Kyle's mother because she has the same tomato-red hair—cheers loudest.

I think if Kyle smiled any harder, his mouth would fall off.

Another woman yells, "That's my Eric!" Eric blushes and his face turns redder than Kyle's hair.

"Ms. Bryce?" asks Principal Klein. "Where are you? Take a bow with your class."

As the audience quiets, I exchange worried looks with Giovanna, who is now standing next to me. My stomach clenches tighter.

"Ms. Bryce? Are you here?" asks Principal Klein. He turns to us and whispers, "Is she in the bathroom?"

Maggie clears her throat and steps forward. She's holding

the letter we agreed to write—one of the two letters we wrote—and she hands it to Principal Klein.

"What's this?" he asks.

"It's from the entire class," she says.

"Should I read it aloud to the audience?" Principal Klein asks, opening the envelope.

"Um, you might want to read it to yourself first," Maggie suggests.

41
MAGGIE

As Principal Klein reads the letter I just handed him, clutching it in his thick, oversized hands, he keeps looking up, staring at us, and then reading again. This happens every half second or so. I have taken several steps back so I blend in with the rest of the class. Although I handed him the letter, we all signed it.

The letter is not long, so I think Principal Klein must have read it a few times. We considered writing a lengthier note but decided short and sweet would be fine.

I pretty much memorized it after Eric wrote it and we all approved it.

Dear Principal Klein,

Ms. Bryce resigned from class two weeks ago and all of us students in Class 507 would like a new teacher, please. We would especially like to have a nice teacher.

But if that's not possible, we'll take whatever teacher we can get.

We're sorry we didn't tell anyone sooner. But we think we learned a lot, even without an adult teaching us. The things we learned weren't really teacher-teaching stuff, anyway.

Sincerely,
Class 507

When he finally finishes reading, Principal Klein lowers the page. He looks at us again, staring at each and every one of us, down the line. Then, he looks out into the audience and clears his throat. The audience is silent, waiting. "We seem to have a problem," he says. He stands there for a few seconds longer, looking at the ceiling and talking to himself, as if trying to find the right words to say.

My legs feel weak. I was confident we were doing the right thing, but now I'm not sure.

All I see is doom.

"It appears Ms. Bryce has chosen an early retirement," our principal says. *"Two weeks ago."* He turns to us. "And what have you been *doing* for the past two weeks?"

We fidget. No one wants to speak up. You wouldn't think eighteen kids and a few hundred people in the audience could be this quiet.

But they can be *very* quiet.

Finally, Eric says, "Well, we wrote this play. And we did homework, too. Like, a lot of homework. And I guess we also goofed off a little."

Principal Klein frowns. "We will get a new teacher, and you will have to make up the last two weeks of class if you want to graduate to middle school after this year." He pauses. "I'm just not sure how you can make up the time." He drums his fingers on his cheek. "I'll need to think about it over winter break."

"I will teach them *over* winter break." It's Ms. Bryce—I would recognize her high, scratchy voice anywhere. She steps into the theater aisle near the back of the room. Apparently, she's been watching the play this whole time and strides toward us. My mouth drops open in surprise.

Amazed, shocked, and stupefied.

I immediately close my mouth. People never look intelligent with their mouths gaping open, and appearances are important.

Ms. Bryce looks younger and prettier than I remember. Maybe the last two weeks without teaching have relaxed her. Or maybe I just remembered her more withered and grouchy than she really was. But she's not smiling. Her expression is stern and serious.

"Where have you been?" asks the principal.

"Just now I was in the bathroom," she replies. "But I will come in over break and ensure these students make up their lost weeks. That should give you enough time to find a permanent substitute teacher when break is over."

"But we have plans to go to Hawaii," says Samantha.

"We're going to visit my grandma," whines Cooper.

"I'm going to visit Harvard," I say.

"Maybe you should have thought of that before you kept this horrible secret," says Principal Klein. "I think the class coming in over break is a marvelous idea. If, of course, the parents agree."

He looks out into the audience. Parents mutter between themselves.

"How about summer school instead?" yells a tall man with a beard.

"What if they stayed an hour later every day for the rest of the year?" suggests a short lady with a long nose.

"I think they should repeat fifth grade!" shouts a big man who looks like an older version of Brian. A chorus of boos immediately meets him. He looks mad, as if he wants to chuck an eraser at someone, and sits down with his arms crossed.

A few more objections ring out, but not as many as I would have thought. A man in the back shouts, "I think coming in over winter break is terrific!"

A few other parents shout out, "Yes!" and "I agree!" Many parents quickly yell similar assents. Other parents nod their heads. Very few of them seem to object.

"Then we will keep class open during winter vacation, except of course on the holidays themselves," says Principal Klein. "I understand some of you might have conflicts. If your child cannot attend, then we can discuss alternate arrangements."

My shoulders slump. Missing our entire winter vacation would be a harsh punishment, but maybe one we deserve.

Warranted, earned, merited, and justified.

I guess visiting Harvard is out the window. But, truly, going to Harvard doesn't sound so great anymore. Harvard can wait.

I'm only in fifth grade. I should try enjoying it more.

Mr. Wolcott wanders onto our stage. I forgot about him, hiding backstage behind the curtain. But there he is, stepping briskly in front of us and looking out into the crowd.

I wonder if he's going to start spouting Shakespeare. I wouldn't be surprised if he starts blabbering lines from *something*.

"Mr. Chips?" asks Principal Klein. "What are you doing here?" But Mr. Wolcott doesn't seem to hear him, or if he does, maybe he's forgotten his stage name. Instead, he continues gazing at the audience, staring as if in a daze.

He's going to perform. I know it. He opens his mouth. He's going to quote something profound yet deeply confusing.

His eyes twinkle. I've never seen eyes twinkle so brightly before. It must be the stage lights.

Wait a second. He's not staring blindly into the audience like I thought. He's peering at one person in particular. He's gawking at Ms. Bryce.

"Franny?" he asks. He stands at the lip of the stage, frozen, as if covered by a thick blanket of ice. "Franny Bree?"

"I go by Frances Bryce now," says our former teacher. "I haven't used my old stage name, Franny Bree, in years." Then her mouth falls open, as if she's seen a ghost. "Willard? Is that you? Truly?"

"Do you remember our play? *Romeo and Juliet*?" Mr. Wolcott's voice creaks with emotion. Tears roll down his cheeks. As he speaks, he waves his hands in the air. "O, speak again, bright angel, for thou art as glorious to this night, being o'er my head, as is a winged messenger of heaven."

Ms. Bryce nods. With her arms waving and her voice cracking, she recites, "O Romeo, Romeo! Wherefore art thou Romeo? Deny thy father and refuse thy name."

It's pure drivel, but Mr. Wolcott hops offstage as if he were suddenly a kid again and rushes to Ms. Bryce. They meet, their arms outstretched, and they seem to melt into each other's arms like a molten chocolate cake.

Mr. Wolcott and Ms. Bryce look oblivious to everyone but each other, ignoring the gasps and points and cries from around the room.

After a moment, they break off their hug, but they

continue holding hands as they skip back up the aisle and toward the theater entrance doors.

I would never have imagined seeing Ms. Bryce skip. I always think of her as stomping angrily. But now she seems lighter than air.

Maybe teachers aren't always who they seem to be in class. Just like my classmates aren't who I thought they were, either.

Apparently, I'm still learning things.

As they arrive at the doors, Ms. Bryce, or maybe I should call her Ms. Bree, turns to us. "I'll see you kids on Monday. And you better be prepared for lots of homework."

A few of us groan. But plenty of homework seems quite fine with me, especially since I won't have to assign it to the class. Honestly, *doing* homework is a lot easier than *creating* homework.

42
KYLE

Mr. Wolcott, who I'll always think of as Mr. Chips, and Ms. Bryce, who I'll probably now always think of as Franny Bree, stroll out of the room hand in hand, staring into each other's eyes. Principal Klein dismisses us with a reminder that we are expected in class on Monday unless our parents make other arrangements.

My family waits for me at their seats. Mom brought all my brothers and sisters to watch. When I approach, little Leah hugs my legs. AJ squirms to get out of Mom's grasp. She puts him down and kisses me on the cheek.

"You wrote that?" Mom asks.

"I had some help," I admit.

"When did you have the time?"

I shrug. "I squeezed it in."

"I thought it was absolutely wonderful. I had no idea you were such a talented writer."

I bite my lip. "So you don't think I'm good for nothing?"

Mom wraps me in a hug. "Oh, honey. Why in the world would you think that? Of course not."

A warm blanket of tingling happiness covers my feet and starts crawling up my legs. My mom's hug lingers. I want to play it cool, so I shrug her off me, but I can't get the smile off my face, even though I try. "Does this mean you'll take that promotion?" I ask.

"I've already turned it down, Kyle." She puts her hands on her hips. "Wait. Is this why you wrote the play? To prove something to me?"

"I don't know. I think I did it mostly to prove something to myself. But—is it too late to change your mind? I bet you'd be great at the job. And I can help out more at home. Like really help out. I'll surprise you."

Mom leans over and kisses me on the cheek. "It wouldn't be a surprise at all. But I don't know. We'll have to see."

"Your show was almost as good as *Squiggle Cat*," says Marley, stepping between Mom and me and smiling.

"It was better!" says Nate.

"Thanks, guys," I say. I can't imagine higher praise from them.

Marley says, "Yow, yow, yow!"

"But we will still need to discuss what your class has been up to," Mom tells me. There's an angry look on her face, but her eyes don't look upset; they look happy. I think I'll be let off without too miserable of a punishment.

School over winter break is punishment enough.

Maggie stands near me. "You did a nice job writing the play, Kyle."

"Thanks." If someone as smart as Maggie compliments you, then you know you did a good job. "I guess I'll see you Monday."

She smiles, and I'm reminded how pretty her smile is, and I wonder if a big oaf like me and a big brain like Maggie could ever be friends.

Stranger things have happened, I guess.

Maggie turns to her parents. Her dad's rapidly wagging finger waves in front of Maggie's frown. His voice is loud and his eyes glare with anger. Maggie's mom pats Maggie on the back, but Maggie looks like she's about to cry.

I bet Maggie is looking forward to coming to school over break.

Funny, I sort of am, too.

"Ready to go home?" asks Mom. She bends down to grab AJ, but then looks up, her eyes wide. "Where's AJ?"

For a brief moment, I panic. Not again! I breathe easier when I see a small foot disappearing under a seat next to me.

I bend down. AJ looks at me from his hiding spot.

I grab him by his arms and hoist him into mine. "I've got him, Mom. I know it's hard to keep an eye on everyone all the time. Even the most responsible people can't always be responsible."

Mom smiles gratefully, takes AJ from me, and hugs him close to her chest. That kid is going to get himself in some serious trouble someday, especially when he learns to walk.

We all head down the aisle to leave when I remember I need to grab my backpack from our classroom. "It'll just be a minute," I assure them.

I lead my family out of the theater, down the corridor, past the lockers, and to our classroom.

"Is any of this artwork yours?" Mom asks, pointing at the bird pictures dotting the hallway.

"No," I admit. "But I'll get something up there soon. Just you watch."

I have a strong urge to draw a picture of a woodpecker.

As we enter the room, Mom says, "So this is where you were keeping your big secret?" I think she's surprised the room is still in good shape and hasn't been burned to the ground or something.

Considering we didn't have a teacher, we took care of things pretty well, if you ask me.

"My backpack is on my desk." My family waits by the door as I hurry to the back of the room.

As I grab my backpack, I hear a soft chirping noise. It almost sounds like someone laughing at me. I listen closely. It's an animal.

"Ready?" Mom asks.

"Wait," I say. "Please. Just wait."

The chattering continues, and I follow the noise to the corner of the room. The sound bounces out from in back of the trash can. I slide it to the side.

Huddled in the corner is Soda, surrounded by crumbs and a half-eaten peanut butter cracker. Soda shivers. "What are you doing here, boy?" I ask. "Um, I mean, girl." Lifting her up, I give Soda a small kiss on the nose. She chatters back to me.

I pet her softly to calm her. I bet she's pretty scared. Then I walk to her cage. I place her gently inside.

"One more minute," I tell Mom. "Before we go, I have to fill her water and food tray, okay?" I throw Soda a wink. "I'll see you Monday."

EPILOGUE

The following day, Ms. Bryce walks to her mailbox and finds a letter inside. Mr. Wolcott reads it with her, as they are having tea and reciting their favorite lines from *Othello*, which is one of Shakespeare's famous plays.

This is what the letter says:

> *Dear Ms. Bryce,*
>
> *We wanted to thank you for being our teacher. We know we were sometimes difficult, sometimes by accident and other times on purpose, but we never realized how much work it is to be a teacher. We do now.*
>
> *We're sorry that you quit. We hope you stop by and visit sometime.*

The entire fifth-grade class signed the letter.

That didn't keep Ms. Bryce from assigning lots of homework that next week. Although maybe she assigned a little less homework than she had planned.

ACKNOWLEDGMENTS

I do most of my writing at home, so I need to thank Lauren, Madelyn, and Emmy for giving me the time and space to do exactly that, even when they desperately need me to kill a spider or to help with homework. But really, mostly, I need to thank them for the inspiration and encouragement they give me. Without their support, nothing else would matter.

I also have to thank everyone at Scholastic, most especially Jody Corbett, whose spark and genius brought this book to life. Joanna Volpe is probably tired of seeing her name appear in various book acknowledgments, but I can't possibly express my gratitude for her passion and support, along with her extraordinary team, of which Jaida Temperly and Danielle Barthel get their own shout-outs.

Lastly, and the phrase "last but not least" is particularly relevant, I need to thank my past teachers, all of whom shaped me as a person and a writer, for good or for bad but mostly for good, I think. I'd like to expressly thank Bill Paul and Anita Duncan, who taught me (together, as a team) in fifth grade (and also, interestingly, in second grade), because I trace my dream to be an author directly to their classroom, when I wrote books for extra credit along with Peter Wagner, next-door neighbor and exceptional fifth-grade monster illustrator. I still have those books, and they're terribly written, although Peter's pictures are very nice, but Mr. Paul and Mrs. Duncan encouraged me anyway, which was beyond generous.

ABOUT THE AUTHOR

Allan Woodrow grew up in Michigan, always wanting to be an author. His teachers told him to write about what he knew, but he quickly discovered he didn't know very much. He didn't know very much for quite a long time. Allan isn't sure he really knows anything more now than he did in elementary school, but he got tired of waiting and decided to start writing anyway. He is the author of *The Pet War* and the Zachary Ruthless series, as well as other books for young readers, written under secret names. His writing also appears in the Scholastic anthology *Lucky Dog: Twelve Tales of Rescued Dogs*.

Allan currently lives near Chicago. For more about Allan and his books, visit his website at www.allanwoodrow.com.